CHANGE ON THE FLY

MAREN MOORE

MAREN MOORE

Cover Design: Cat with TRC Designs

Formatting: Maren Moore

Photographer: Wander Aguir Photography

Model: Andrew Biernat

Editing: Rebecca's Fiarest Reveiws

CHANGE ON THE FLY

For all the girls who have loved someone in secret.
This one's for you.

MAREN MOORE

PLAYLIST

Heat Waves- Glass Animals
Shivers- Ed Sheeran
Messy Acoustic- Chase Rice
Memory- Kane Brown, blackbear
Chasing Stars- Alesso, Mashmello, James Bay
There was this Girl- Riley Green
Miss You a Little- Bryce Vine, lovelytheband
Leave Before You Love Me- Marshmello, Jonas Brothers

Full playlist on Spotify

MAREN MOORE

CHAPTER ONE
REED

There are a lot of perks to being a professional hockey player. Hell, an athlete in general. Besides the money, the fame, the endorsements. The free shit that sports companies throw at you.

And one of those perks is currently perched on my lap, trailing her hot pink manicured finger up my chest.

Her name is Elizabeth. And honestly, I'm surprised I even remember her name because our entire interaction at Liam and Juliet's wedding lasted about fifteen minutes in a cramped bathroom stall and there was definitely no talking done. Or any talking during any of the times after that.

You see, I'm the kind of guy that enjoys the finer things in life… without all of the complications that people seem to add. Why make anything hard when it's already sweet? I'm twenty-eight and living my dream, playing hockey for one of the best teams in the country. I've got the most beautiful women at my fingertips, fans who adore me, and then I have my ma and my sister Emery. Nothing to hold me back and *no one* to answer to. And that's exactly how I want it.

Seriously, life is *good*.

"Has anyone told you tonight that you are the most beautiful girl in the entire room?" I say to the busty blonde in my lap. Her plump, bright red lips stretch into a wide, confident grin. It's not a lie, she is gorgeous. It's just part of the game. You say what they want to hear, and everyone's happy.

"That's because I'm the *only* girl in the room, Reed Davidson." She giggles before tossing her long, sleek hair over her tan shoulder that peeks out from her sleeveless dress.

I grin cheekily, revealing the dimple that always seals the deal. Just as I'm leaning in, Briggs, my best friend, walks up and flops down onto the couch next to us. I shoot him a look that says "get the fuck out of here, cockblocker," but Briggs being Briggs, doesn't pick up on the signal.

"Tonight sucks," he mutters. He's nursing a still full beer, and moping around the bar like he's lost his puppy dog.

Sighing heavily, I nudge blondie from my lap and thankfully, she takes the hint and scampers off back toward her group of friends, leaving me alone with Briggs.

"Alright, what's up? What are you cryin' in your beer about?"

His jaw clenches at my jab, but he just shakes his head, staring off into the distance. Best forward in the NHL or not, the guy is dramatic and broody as shit. I've just learned to live with it, and fuck with him any chance I get.

"Briggs."

"Just some shit."

Another blasé answer. A Briggs's specialty.

I pull my phone from my pocket and swipe away the unopened texts from puck bunnies who text me weekly for a hookup, and instead, I go straight to my other best friend, Liam's text and open it. He's sent a photo of him, Juliet and the girls on the beach. The girls are posing next to a sandcastle as big as they are, and it brings a genuine smile to my face. Liam and I have been best friends for as long as I can remember. We played hockey together, until he became the coach of the Avalanche last year. Now that he's married to Juliet, he's coaching high school hockey and I miss seeing him and the girls as much as I used to.

They've been in the Bahamas for over a week, while I'm stuck here babysitting Briggs. I can't wait for the girls to get home to tell me all about their vacation.

I love those two sassy girls. Being their uncle Reed is one of the best things in my life. But me as a dad? The last thing I could ever see myself as is a father *or* a husband, or anything even close. As much as I love Ari and Ken... I love bringing them back to Liam at the end of the night, so I can go out with the boys, catch a game, enjoy the single unattached life.

I'm a perpetual bachelor, and that's *exactly* how I plan to stay.

Which is why Broody Briggs, myself, Asher, Hudson and Graham are at a bar on a Tuesday night... because, why not? We're all single, hot professional hockey players with no one to go home to, so why not spend it out on the town with a few beers? We all play together for the Chicago Avalanche, and it's the best job on the damn planet.

When people say, "do what you love and you'll never work a day in your life," it's true. Sometimes it's hard to believe that I get to wake up and play hockey for a living, but at the same time, I busted my ass to be here. I worked from sun up to sun down to be the player I am today.

To celebrate another great practice, we decided to come out tonight for a night of bunnies and booze. Except, as of late, things have been... less exciting, since Briggs is walking the straight and narrow or he's off the team. He's been in more fights the past six months than I have in my entire hockey career.

So, to make sure that he stays out of trouble, that he doesn't find himself in front of a pap's camera, or worse, stuck in a jail cell for another night, I'm stuck babysitting until further notice.

Hockey player or hockey-player nanny? That is the real question.

The rest of the night passes uneventfully, thanks to Briggs's sour mood. Asher, Hudson and Graham each found a puck bunny for the night and dipped out before midnight, leaving me and Briggs alone, so I decide to cut out as well.

"I'm headed out, you want a ride?" I ask Briggs, who's rapid-fire typing on his phone.

He doesn't answer me, so I punch him in the shoulder to get his attention.

"Fuck, what was that for?"

"Dude, you're in a *bar* and have been glued to your phone all night. I'm out, you need a ride?"

He shakes his head no. "I'll call an Uber later."

"Stay out of shit, dude, seriously. I'm not bailing you out of jail, and please, for God's sake, wrap it up. We don't need miniature versions of you skating around." I grin, teasing him.

The dick nods, barely acknowledging me, eyes still focused on his phone. Asshole. I down the rest of my beer and leave the bottle on the table, with a few bills I pull from my wallet, and then make my way out of the bar. Thankfully, we frequent this place often, and the owner lets us use the back door, so we can avoid fans and the media. As much as I love having my picture taken, I'm not a fan of the paps.

I open the back door of the building and step outside into the cool night air, inhaling a deep breath before I begin walking across the pavement to find my truck in the sea of vehicles. Just as I'm about to unlock it, my phone rings in my pocket. I fish it out and see it's Holland, my sister's best friend.

Weird. Why would she be calling me after midnight?

I swipe and answer, "You know that they say any calls after ten are booty calls, right?"

"Reed?" She all but yells into the phone. The music in the background is so damn loud I can hardly hear her.

"Holland? What's up? You realize it's after midnight?"

I unlock my truck and jump inside, starting the engine.

"Uh, well, something happened." Her words are muffled. The connection sounds like shit, and I can barely hear what she's saying. "Can you come get us, please? We're at Sorority Row."

I've known Holland since we were kids and never once has she asked me to pick her or Emery up anywhere, since they generally Uber everywhere. It makes me worried that something happened.

"Are you and Emery safe?"

"Yes. Emery just… had a *tiny* bit too much tonight," she mutters.

"I'll be there in ten. Where are you?"

"Upstairs bathroom." A second later, I hear the sound of heaving. Great, Emery's drunk as shit. I make a mental note to grab a bucket at the sorority house.

I slam my truck into drive and pull out of the parking lot opposite the club. Thank fuck I'm downtown, and not at home, because this drive would've taken twice as long. Sorority Row is only ten minutes from the bar.

My tires ramp up the curb when I come to a stop then park, not bothering to even shut the truck off before I hop out and stalk up the steps of the house. By the looks of it, there's a massive party happening, and it makes my blood boil. I hate my sister going here. I know this is where entitled, rich douchebags party, and I want Emery nowhere near them. Especially since I can't have eyes on her.

I'm a big brother, sue me. I've always protected her and it's not any different now that she's an adult.

Once I'm inside the house, there's people everywhere dressed in togas and skimpy lingerie. I've spent many nights here, pre-NHL days, and I know exactly what tonight's about. It's rush week. The craziest week of the entire year, where everyone is doing whatever they can to be selected to pledge. There's fighting, hazing, a bunch of shit they shouldn't be doing. Meaning, my little sister shouldn't fucking be here.

I push through a crowd of people, trying to make my way to the stairwell.

A guy, wearing a toga, steps in front of me as I'm about to climb the stairs, and I run smack into him.

Damnit.

"Holy shit! You're Reed Davidson, can I have a photo, man?"

"Sorry, dude, I'm looking for someone." I sidestep him then take the stairs two at a time and make my way down the hallway until I find the bathroom. When I swing the last door to the right open, I find my sister sitting on the edge of the bathtub, mascara streaking down her cheeks and a drunken grin.

"Oh, it's my brother, lovely," she slurs. "What the hell are you doing here?"

She drops her head in her hands and groans obnoxiously loud. "He always ruins my buzz."

Well damn, I'm hurt. Sorry I have to be the semi-responsible one of the two of us.

"Went a lil' hard tonight, did ya, Em?" I tease.

My eyes drift to Holland, who's leaning against the vanity wearing a worried expression. I get it. Em's shitfaced and puking everywhere, but it's nothing some painkillers and water can't cure.

Em looks up at me and grins. "Well, someone has to have fun

for the both of us. You're kinda a stick in the mud now."

"Nah, baby sis, I just don't like getting trashed and then puking in the sorority girls' toilet."

She flips me the middle finger with her black manicured nail, but laughs, which quickly turns into a moan. "Shit, my head. There's two of you. Why are there two of you? I can barely handle one."

Holland throws her head back and laughs, and I narrow my eyes at her then Emery.

"You know, for being your knight in shining armor, you two sure are mouthy."

Holland rolls her eyes and looks like she's going to say something, but Emery speaks up instead. "My jerk of a frat douchebag boooooyfriend broke up with me so we took looooots of shots. Lots and lots of shots. I lost count."

"Thank fuck, I thought I was gonna have to beat the shit out of the guy to get rid of him."

"Shut up. He was nice… and smart."

I laugh. "Yeah, just your type."

I'm sure Em gets sick of my teasing, but it's what we do. We talk shit to each other like it's our religion. If Emery wasn't talking shit to me on the daily, I'd think something was wrong.

"So, you want me to help you up or do you plan on sleeping here tonight?"

"I'm becoming one with the floor." She groans.

I reach down and lift her off her feet, and she stands shakily on her heels. I toss my arm over her shoulder to steady her.

"Please do not puke in my truck or I'm leaving you on the side of the road."

"Ha ha, very funny."

I stop dead and look at her. "I'm serious."

Even though I'm not. I chuckle and take the damp rag that Holland is holding out for me then wipe Em's face. Em's got her eyes closed and she's looking a bit green, so I do her the favor of wiping some of the smeared makeup and dried throw up off, before handing it back to Holland.

Growing up, I'd been the one Em called when she needed someone. We didn't have a dad, so she had me. I changed her tires in high school and beat the shit out of the guy that called her a slut after she wouldn't sleep with him.

I've always done whatever I could to protect her, that's what I'm here for. When we were kids, she'd follow me around and do everything that I did. She had a stick in her hand at five years old and could skate circles around most of my friends, even though we were eight and twice as big as her. My entire life she's been my shadow and I guess there could be a worse best friend than your baby sister.

We walk out of the sorority house, down the concrete driveway and when we get to my truck, I pick Emery up and put her in the passenger seat.

She moans and groans the entire time, like she's losing a damn limb.

"Sheesh, you're dramatic."

"Runs in the family, I guess."

I scoff. "That is about enough out of you tonight." I grab the bucket Holland thought to grab and put it in Em's lap then shut the door, silencing her protest.

When I'm done, I turn to Holland. Her deep blue eyes are filled with amusement at my expense, not Emery's. She loves our banter.

Her arms are wrapped around her torso, hugging herself. For Christ's sake, I didn't even realize she had this tiny top on; she's got to be freezing. For some reason, at this moment, it dawns on me that I've never really... noticed Holland as anything other than my little sister's best friend, until right now. Maybe it's because she's dressed in a crop top that shows more cleavage than I've ever seen her with or because the skirt she's wearing makes me want to cover her up so no one can see how short it is. Or it could be the way that her legs look paired with those heels. Even though they've gotta be five-inches tall, she's still at least half a foot, if not shorter, than me. Her long, blonde hair falls past her chest to her waist.

Fuck, she's *gorgeous.*

That's the last thing I should be thinking about, yet here we are. I've watched her grow from a boy-band crazed teenager into... this beautiful *woman.*

A woman who is so off-limits, it's not even funny.

What the hell are you thinking, Davidson?

Get your shit together.

I clear my throat. "You cool with crashing at my place tonight?

I'm sure Ma wouldn't appreciate me dropping off the brat at her house tonight in her drunken state."

Holland nods. "Yeah, I can go get my car tomorrow. Uh, could you possibly help me into the truck?" She looks down at her skirt, nervously. "This skirt and these shoes..."

Yeah, I can't imagine she'd be able to get in there without flashing me and the world what's underneath it. Not like I'd complain right now...

What? I'm a guy.

"Yeah, of course." I place my hands on her waist, ignoring the feel of her silky skin beneath my touch, and hoist her into the back seat of the truck. Definitely not taking a glimpse at her ass as she did so.

Nope. Absolutely not. I wouldn't. Scout's honor.

"Fuck," I mutter to myself. This is bad. Obviously I should've picked a bunny and gone home with her, since I'm suddenly lusting after my little sister's best friend.

It's probably just an off night, and definitely a fluke.

Definitely.

Em falls asleep before I even pull away from the curb. She's slumped awkwardly against the window, drool pooling in the corner of her mouth. I should snap a picture, so I can torture her with it later.

I grin at the thought.

The entire drive back to my house, I force myself to focus on the road, and not drag my eyes to the rearview mirror where

Holland's perched in the back seat, directly in my line of vision.

I only stole a few glances, and I didn't think she noticed until our eyes connected in the mirror and something... different passes through our gaze.

Fuck, what is happening?

Tearing my gaze from hers, I fumble with the radio and turn it up to distract myself for the remainder of the drive. Once I pull into the driveway and come to a stop, Emery flies forward and her eyes pop open.

"What happened? What did I miss?"

Holland laughs her ass off at Emery's sudden outburst, and then Em's slumping back against the seat and letting out a soft snore.

"I'm not claiming her," I mutter as I hop out of the truck, then open Holland's door. She places her hand in mine and I help her out before going around to grab Em. It's a whole damn production to get her into the house and up the stairs, but thank fuck, Holland takes over once we make it to the guest room.

They disappear through the door, and I head to my room and take a lightning-fast shower and throw on a pair of grey sweats and a faded black tee before walking back out to the hallway. Holland's leaning against the wall next to the door, scrolling on her phone. She's shed the heels and is standing barefoot now.

"Hey, uh, do you need something to sleep in? I have a shirt and some boxers I can give you?"

She jumps, clearly startled. "Holy crap, I didn't even hear you come up. Yes, that would be great."

I nod, and go back to my room, grabbing her an old hockey shirt and a pair of boxers. This is the first time since probably high school that I've slept in the same house as Holland, and it definitely feels nothing like it did back then.

Walking back out to the hallway, I hand her the clothes, and she smiles shyly before taking them from me.

"Shower's over there. If you need something, just let me know."

"Thanks, Reed. I mean for letting us stay here, but also thanks for coming to get us."

I shrug. "It's nothing. I'd rather pick you two up then have you take an Uber home when Em can hardly hold her head up. I appreciate that you thought enough to call me. Night, Holland."

"Goodnight."

I walk back toward my room and I hear the guest bathroom door shut behind me and the water turn on. And now what am I definitely not going to do? Think about her naked on the other side of that door.

That's what I tell myself for the next two hours as I toss and turn. From one side to the other, sleep evading me. I put my pillow over my head and groan. Finally, I just give up.

Fuck it. When you can't sleep... the remedy is always cereal.

Don't tell my coach that, and definitely not the trainer, but sugar cures everything. Especially in high doses of Captain Crunch.

My secret though.

I toss the blanket aside and crack my door open quietly, careful not to wake Em and Holl, and tiptoe down the hallway into the kitchen. I grab a bowl, the box of cereal from the pantry and open the fridge to get the milk.

"Reed?" A whispered voice comes from behind me, scaring the fuck out of me so badly that I send the milk flying across the island, where it lands with a wet squelch, puddling around the now-busted carton.

Goddamnit.

Holland's staring at me with wide eyes. Her hair is down and messy, obviously disheveled from sleep.

"Holy fuck, Holland, you scared the shit out of me!" I grunt. My heart's still racing in my chest.

Damn Reed, you're turning into a pussy.

She starts laughing, quietly at first, placing her hand over her mouth when she sees the milk spilled on the floor.

"I'm so... sor-ry," she says through her laugh. I walk across the room to where both she and the milk are, grabbing the towel from the counter before bending down to clean it up.

Then her laugh is gone, replaced by a sharp hiss, and when I look up and see her thick thighs staring back at me, I realize what she's wearing...

Nothing but my t-shirt and fuck, nothing has ever looked so good. The dark shirt hits her mid-thigh, covering all of the good stuff, still leaving enough covered for my imagination to do the rest.

I clear my throat and stand abruptly, not wanting to make her uncomfortable, and she steps back.

"Shit, I'm sorry, Holland, I didn't realize."

"No, it's okay. I'm sorry."

We both speak at the same time.

"Uh, sometimes when I can't sleep... I eat a bowl of-"

Before I can finish, she says, "Cereal?"

I grin. "You remember?"

She nods then smiles slightly. "You would wake up all the time just to eat Captain Crunch. At some point, Em started to call you 'Captain' behind your back."

"She would. I guess the tradition kind of carried over to adulthood. Not nearly as fun, though, as when I was sneaking around to eat it in the middle of the night."

My hopes of cereal are gone since the only milk I had is in a puddle on the floor, but suddenly, I'm not sorry that it happened.

"So, looks like no Captain Crunch tonight, but I've got... Pop-Tarts," I offer. For a professional athlete, I probably shouldn't have this much sugar in my kitchen, but I keep my body in the best condition I can, so it generally doesn't become an issue.

I get us both a Pop-Tart from the pantry then put the box back inside. She's sitting at the bar now with her chin in her hand. Not a lick of makeup on, and damn, she's beautiful. And for the second time tonight, even though I know I shouldn't, I realize just how much of a woman she's become.

Somehow, I never noticed it. I never let myself notice it. I probably shouldn't now, but I do.

And that's how the rest of the night is spent, talking about nothing with Holland, eating a Pop-Tart, and for the very first time, I realize that I might be in some seriously deep shit.

CHAPTER TWO

REED

My phone ringing jolts me awake. I don't even try to open my eyes as I reach out and blindly feel for my phone on my nightstand. Once I finally feel it, I crack one eye open and see Briggs's name on the screen and groan.

Damnit, Briggs. I slide my thumb across and answer, "You better be in jail or dying." My voice is semi-muffled since I'm face down in bed.

"Why the fuck haven't you answered your phone?"

I glance at the glowing blue numbers on my alarm clock. Four thirty-six.

What the fuck?

"Well, Asshole, it is only four-thirty in the morning, so like a normal person, I was asleep. Why are you even awake right now?"

"Your mom called me."

I pull myself up with that statement. "What? Why would my mom call you? Damn, I was sleeping so hard, I didn't hear the phone till now."

"I don't know, man, she said it was important and she couldn't reach you. Call her now."

Shit, shit, shit. My mind immediately goes to Emery. After the past few days she's had, I hope she's okay.

"Fuck, okay. Thanks."

I sit up fully now, gathering my bearings for a second. I was sleeping hard as hell after an extra grueling practice. Every muscle in my damn body hurts today, even more than normal. I dial Mom's number, and she answers on the first ring.

"Reed. Thank God," she breathes.

I run my hand through my hair, still trying to wake up. "Yeah, Ma, what's up? Everything okay? It's the middle of the night."

"I just got a call from your father."

Unease creeps up my spine at the mention of Robert. Neither Emery nor I have seen him since I was eight and to say he's a sore subject is an understatement, one we don't usually broach. I have no idea why he'd be trying to reach me, especially not at four thirty-six in the damn morning.

"Why is Robert calling you in the middle of the night?" Just saying his name leaves a bitter taste in my mouth.

"I'm not sure, honey, he wouldn't say. He said that it's extremely urgent that he speaks with you. And to please try and have you call as soon as possible."

"This makes no sense. He's never tried to reach out before. What could he possibly have to say to me right now? Or period, Ma?"

I hear the hesitation in her voice. "Sweetheart, I know. I know you harbor a lot of ill feelings for him, but I can tell something is wrong. I was married to him for a long time, and I could hear it in his voice. I'm not saying you have to call him, that decision is completely up to you, but I do think that it's important or he wouldn't be reaching out to me in order to get in touch with you."

I drag my hand down my face, the lull of sleep is finally gone, and now my heart is pounding inside my chest like a sledgehammer. I haven't spoken to Robert in years. Since I was a child. Yet, the sting of his abandonment and betrayal still feels fresh. The thought of speaking to him causes dread to form heavy in my stomach. Why now?

What happened to prompt this call? Unease creeps up my throat until it feels like it's too much to swallow back down.

"I don't know if I can talk to him, Ma, not after everything. After he left us."

"I know, honey, I... I could just hear the pain and panic in his voice. It's been a long time, but I know him."

I sigh, dragging in a ragged breath. The last thing I expected when I called her was to hear this. My chest feels tight with anxiousness. "Can you send me his number in a text? I'll try. Once. Thanks, Ma."

"I love you, honey," she says softly. "Never forget that."

Right now, I wish I was with her. I can't imagine what it feels like for her, speaking to him for the first time since he left us. I'm sure her old wounds have broken open, just as they have for me.

We end the call, and a few seconds later, my phone chimes

with a number.

The number is daunting; it's big and bold, causing anger, familiar and sharp, to swirl deep in my gut, but I push it aside. I hit the digits and wait for the phone to ring.

"Hello?" A deep baritone comes through the speaker, the same one I remember from my childhood, even though so many times I wish I could've forgotten it.

Fuck, it hits me straight in the chest.

I clear my throat that's clogged with emotion. Pain, sadness, regret. So many emotions, I can't seem to sift through them all. "It's Reed."

He exhales loudly, like my phone call is what he had been waiting for. "Reed... son-"

"Don't call me your son," I spit, cutting him off. I rise from my bed and start to pace the room. Desperate for a way to burn off the anxiety threatening to close my throat completely.

Fuck, I'm not prepared to confront a demon, not without warning, which makes it difficult to work through the thoughts clamoring in my head.

"I'm sorry. I needed your information to give to Children and Family Services." He begins hacking on the other end of the line, causing me to pause. I'm trying to gather my wits, to calm down. But it's not working very well.

"Why would DCFS need to contact *me*?" My anger morphs into confusion.

"I'm not sure how to say this, Reed." He starts to softly cry on the other end of the phone. "Your sister, Amelia, and her husband, Adam, were killed this morning in a robbery gone wrong in New York City. They have a son, Evan." Robert's voice breaks as he speaks. It seems unreal to hear emotion in his voice, to hear him so affected, even though, logically, he did just lose his daughter.

Amelia's... *dead?* My half-sister, who I've only met twice, briefly, is... dead. Shock hits me full force. I knew something was off for Robert to reach out to me for the first time in twenty years, but I never expected this.

Part of me is sad. Sad that my sister's life ended tragically and that her son will have to grow up without a mother, and sad that I didn't have the opportunity to truly know her. Because of our father, we never had a relationship and that's a regret that I'll have to carry. I could've reached out; I could've pushed the past aside and tried to make amends with her. But now it's too late.

Shit, Evan... *my nephew.* God, I have a fucking nephew. I didn't even know he existed.

"Was the child there? Is he okay?" I ask.

"Evan was at the babysitter's when it happened."

This is all so fucking much to process; my head is spinning. I squeeze my eyes shut, trying to breathe. I can't remember the last time I felt like this.

My sister is dead.

And because of the issues with our father, I didn't have the chance to know her.

"What does this mean? What should I do?"

Robert pauses. "I... I have cancer, Reed. I won't sugarcoat anything. Legally, Evan would become mine, but I'm dying and unfit to be Evan's guardian. I have stage four lung cancer."

The irony of his words isn't lost on me. Kind of like he was unfit to be our parent? So he left when it wasn't fun for him any longer. Emery was younger when he left, so she doesn't feel as deeply or as strongly as I do about him. Emery barely remembers him. But I do. I remember my father walking out, and the feeling of betrayal I felt as he found another wife and had another child when he had abandoned his two other children. Imagine waking up on Christmas morning, knowing your father was with his new family, and you were just an afterthought. He never called. He never sent letters. Once he left, he never tried to see us again. It was clear the choice that he made.

My entire life was spent wondering what I did wrong, what I could have done to make my father stay. To want our family. To want me.

As an adult, I finally realized that it was Robert's issues. I've spent years working through the fucked-up trauma he's left behind.

Now, he's dying. Cancer. It may seem cold to be this unaffected, but the truth is, I mourned the loss of my father a long time ago. That doesn't mean that the pain doesn't blossom somewhere deep inside, it just means that I can't miss someone who's been dead to me since I was eight years old.

"Sorry to hear it," I mutter. I don't trust myself to say anything else right now. Emotions are high, and it's getting harder to swallow by the second.

I wish I wasn't having this conversation. I wish my sister dying wasn't the only reason that my father was reaching out. Most of all, I wish he had realized his mistakes before he was on his deathbed, and actually tried to make it right. If not for me, then for Em.

"My... My wife passed away from breast cancer three years ago. Amelia's mother, and there isn't anyone else aside from you and Emery. You're the oldest, so the choice will be yours. DCSF will be in touch with you, Reed. I wanted to tell you this news myself." He pauses, and I hear a quiet sniffle in the background. "I'm sorry I didn't do right by you or your sister, Reed. I've made a lot of mistakes in my lifetime, and hurting you two is my greatest one. I'm sorry."

With that, my phone beeps. When I look down at the glowing screen, the call has ended, and I'm left staring at a blank display.

I'm still in shock and disbelief that my sister is dead and that I just spoke to Robert for the first time in twenty years. I walk into the kitchen and flick the light on, illuminating the open dining room and kitchen before grabbing a Gatorade from the fridge where I down it in a single gulp.

It does nothing to help the lump still lodged in my throat.

My phone rings again, only this time the caller ID reads New York, NY.

"Hello?"

"Mr. Davidson?" a woman asks. Her voice is raspy, like she's smoked a pack a day for the last thirty years.

"Yes?"

"This is Connie with the Department of Children and Family Services in New York City. I'm sorry to call this early, but there's an emergency. Amelia and Adam Farley passed away tonight, leaving their son, Evan. Right now, he's currently in the custody of DCFS, but we are reaching out to you about placement. You are the next of kin in Amelia's family, as her husband, Adam, has no living relatives that we are able to locate. From my understanding, he was a child of the foster system as well."

My throat runs dry. "Okay. I just spoke with Robert. Is he okay?"

"Right now, he is. He's only three, so he doesn't have a full grasp on what is happening. That might be both a blessing and a curse. Mr. Davidson, I'm very sorry for your loss. I have spoken with your father, and it has been determined that he is unable to care for Evan because he is terminally ill. If the next of kin is not an able caregiver, we move to the next in line. We always look at the available relatives and try to place the minor in the most stable and fit home possible. It seems as if you are the next in line for guardianship as his uncle. You have the choice to accept the responsibility or you may decline."

Holy. Fuck. This cannot be happening. Sweat forms on my brow, and I wipe it away with the back of my hand. The kitchen seems to spin around me, so I grip the counter, frozen in place. Shit just got way more real with this phone call.

"But, I- I... I've never even met this child. I didn't even know about him until ten minutes ago."

Connie pauses, and I hear paperwork shuffling around in the background. "I understand, but aside from Mr. Davidson, you are the child's only stable next of kin. If you decline to take Evan, he will become a ward of the state and be placed in foster care. It seems your sister Emery is not financially-able to care for Evan, which would mean Evan would ultimately have no other option."

While I hear everything the woman is saying, my brain refuses to process it. Instead, my stomach clenches and knots. Sweat drips down my forehead while my clammy hand struggles to keep hold of my phone.

"The choice is yours, Mr. Davidson, but please understand the dire circumstances. You are his only option."

"Ma'am, I hear what you are saying. Loud and clear. I just... there has to be someone else to take him."

"You are the next and only living relative, aside from your father and sister. We cannot place a child in a temporary home with someone who has a terminal illness. Or with a guardian who lives with someone and has no paying job. Evan will remain in the care of the state tonight, but we will need an answer from you within twenty-four hours, Mr. Davidson. I know this is a lot to process, and I apologize for having to be the one to deliver this news, but it's my job to make sure Evan will have a safe place now that his parents are deceased. You have my number, please call me once you've made your decision."

I mumble a half-hearted thank you, and drop my phone onto the counter.

I can't believe this. Any of it. Amelia, Robert dying, Evan... All of it seems unreal.

I have a feeling that this phone call just changed the rest of my life. Fuck.

CHAPTER THREE
REED

The first place I go, after my life is unequivocally rocked, is to Ma's. I can't make a decision like this without her and Emery's input. I wish I could say the decision is an easy one. It'd probably make me a better man if I did. The kind of man who wouldn't have to even think about making this decision. A man who would selflessly take in his deceased sister's child, even though he's never met him.

The same sister he's estranged from and would probably be the very last person she'd want to take care of her child. How could she? She didn't know me. Meeting someone at a coffee shop twice isn't enough time to build a relationship. To gauge the kind of man I am, or the man that I was back then.

All that aside, I don't know what the hell to do with a kid. I mean sure, yeah, I take the girls to the park sometimes and put them to bed for Liam. But being Uncle Reed is a lot different than having a child as your full-time responsibility. Being a parent means you and you alone are responsible for whether or not your child becomes a decent human being, and if that isn't the most overwhelming pressure in the fucking world, I don't know what is.

That's why I've spent the past three hours going over every possible scenario in my head. I'm not the kinda guy to make a rash decision and knowing that a child's life hangs in the balance... honestly, it's fucking with my head.

What if I do it wrong? What if I am the worst parent ever... like my dad? What if I become the very thing I hate most about who he was? Someone who ran at the first sign of trouble. Who wasn't ready to commit to being a parent.

It's not like it's a dog and I can return it to whatever shelter I adopted it from.

It's a child. A living, breathing child who would depend on me to survive. To grow into being a man by learning all the things my mother taught me.

This is going to change the rest of my life.

Two choices: Yes or no.

Either one will determine the trajectory of my future. And his.

"I know this isn't easy for you, honey. But, if it's any consolation, I think you'd be amazing at it... being his guardian." Ma looks at me and gives me a small smile. I'm sitting between her and Emery on a couch that sags with the weight of all three of us.

That's the thing about my ma. Never mind that I'm a professional hockey player with a multi-million-dollar contract and could replace this entire house and then some for her. She says this old, worn-out couch is one where memories were made. Right along with the rest of her small cottage-style house that my childhood was spent in. Growing up, we didn't have much. Not after Robert left.

Sure, he paid Ma child support and that helped, but raising two kids, paying a mortgage, bills, a car note... it was a lot for her. Not to mention the fact that I always needed new gear, and Emery was in dance and cheer and fifty other extra-curriculars. It didn't matter; Ma, somehow, found a way and she never let us know that she struggled. Not till we were older.

Now, looking back, I realize that there were worry lines in the corners of her eyes as she shelled out money for things that she really couldn't afford. All for us. I want to give her the world because she sacrificed selflessly for us.

"Ma, I don't know anything about kids. How can I be responsible for one? I don't know the first thing about them. What about hockey? I mean shit, I live in a house that doesn't have a lick of childproofing. He's barely three, kids his age need childproofing, right?"

Emery laughs, elbowing my side. "You're basically a kid yourself, Reed, how are you going to raise one?"

"Thanks, Em. I feel even better now."

"Oh hush, Emery," Ma chides, "Reed, I know what you're afraid of. And I want you to get it out of your head."

"Impossible."

"It *is* possible. You are nothing like him." She takes my hand in hers and brings her other hand to my cheek. "You are a good man. I know because I raised you that way. Not only do you have the biggest heart of anyone I know, you are kind, compassionate, selfless."

"Mom, stop before he gets an even bigger ego." Em groans.

I chuckle.

Leave it to Emery to make me laugh in a situation like this. Although, being surrounded by Ma and her, it makes me feel less... I don't know, alone while having to decide something of this magnitude. While Emery and I didn't have a father growing up, we had Ma, who was the strongest, most hardworking woman I've ever known.

"I just don't want you to let him have any bearing on your decision, regardless of the past. Look, honey, I forgave your father a long time ago."

I go to speak, but she holds up her hand, stopping me. "I'm not asking you to do the same. Reed, I carried so much anger, hate and pain inside my heart that it was hurting me. Not him, but *me*. I had to learn how to let go and how to move forward or I would never get rid of those feelings I was harboring. I finally realized that while he may have left, he's the one that lost out. He missed seeing you both grow into the amazing adults you are now."

Shit, is someone cutting an onion in here?

"Make the decision from your heart, Reed. Don't let your feelings toward your father impact this one. He doesn't deserve to have any place in it. And no matter what you choose... I will be here to support you."

After I leave Ma and Emery, I head straight for Liam's house. If anyone has good advice, it's Liam. He's been my best friend since we were both drafted, and he's been by my side through everything important in my life, and I've done the same for him.

I pull my truck into his driveway and put it in park, then hop out and walk up to the house. Before I'm even to the front door, it swings open and my girls are running down the driveway in princess tiaras, frilly pink nightgowns and their signature Olaf slippers.

"Uncle Reed! You're here!" Ari screams.

Kennedy launches herself into my arms and squeezes my neck so tight I can't actually breathe.

"How are my girls?"

"Juliet has been painting our nails and now we gotta go to bed, but I missed you so much."

Ari hugs my leg and puts her feet on mine, and I carry all three of us up the driveway while they giggle. Although they aren't my nieces by blood, they're my nieces all the same. When Liam's wife left him, when Ari was only a toddler and Kennedy a baby, I stepped up and did whatever I could. Learned how to change diapers, how to make a bottle, how to pat their backs so they would burp.

We spent the majority of our time calling Liam's mom and

pleading with his sister to take mercy on us. But... we did that shit. And Liam excelled at it. He's the best dad I've ever seen. Then, he met Juliet and everything changed, but for the better. They recently got married and, of course, I was the best man.

I walk through the door and Juliet's standing in the foyer smiling. "These girls. They couldn't wait another second for you to walk through the door." She pulls Ari off my leg then tickles her stomach, causing her to giggle even more. "C'mon girls, let's get you two to bed. Liam's outside on the patio."

"Thanks, Juliet."

It's crazy how much things have changed since he and Juliet got together. How much Liam has changed. He's opened up and he's happier than I've ever seen him.

And I'm so fucking happy for him. If anyone deserves happiness, it's him. And Ari and Kennedy are ridiculously happy, and that's what matters most.

When I walk out the back door, I find Liam at the table, nursing a beer.

"What's up, stranger?"

I sit down in the patio chair opposite him and run my hands through my hair. "Sorry I haven't been by. Things got complicated quickly."

His eyebrows rise in surprise. "Yeah? What happened?"

"My sister, Amelia, the one from Robert's second marriage? Her and her husband... they were killed in a robbery in New York."

It still feels unreal to say it out loud, and even more insane that

I'm sitting here about to ask Liam for the most important advice of my life.

"Holy shit, Reed, I'm sorry."

I nod. "Thank you. It's a weird feeling. Like she's my sister, even though I barely knew her, and it hurts, man. It hurts to know that I didn't do more to make that relationship work. And then I spoke with Robert for the first time in years."

Liam sits up in his chair. "How'd that go?"

"As expected, he was the one who broke the news that Amelia passed away. He seemed genuinely upset and emotional. Fuck, I was emotional. It was so much at once, ya know? But that's not even the most shocking part." I stand from the chair and walk over to the cooler, grabbing a beer. I twist the top off and take a long sip.

"They have a son. Evan. And Robert has cancer. Stage Four."

"Reed, fuck man, that's a lot. I'm sorry."

I look down at the beer cap in my hand as I run my thumb along the jagged edge. "I'm the next of kin for this kid, Liam. They want me to take him, be his legal guardian. Technically, it's Robert, but he's terminally ill. They won't place Evan in his care."

"Wow."

I nod. "I mean fuck, Liam, what am I supposed to do? If I don't accept then he's going to go into the system. A group home or foster care. I can't imagine doing that to him. I think about my dad and what it was like to grow up without one. If I say no, then I'm essentially leaving this kid without his parents or his family."

Liam exhales. "That's a big decision. You know it as well as I do. You remember what it was like being a single dad to the girls. Shit, I barely kept my head above water. If it wouldn't have been for you, then I wouldn't have made it."

"Yeah, but I don't know how to be a parent. Sure, I helped out when I could, but raising one? His life being solely in my hands? That seems like a responsibility that's... I don't know, fucking scary."

I drag my hand down my face. It's not an easy decision, but something in the pit of my stomach tells me if I say no and don't help him, I'll be doing the wrong thing. Abandoning him the way my father abandoned me.

"Fuck yeah... parenting is scary. There's no doubt about it. And you know it doesn't get easier as time goes on. Yeah, you learn a little more as you go, but it's like walking around in the dark with a blindfold and hoping you don't fuck everything up. But with that being said, Reed, you'd be an amazing guardian to that kid."

My stomach dips at his words. It feels weird to hear them, for this to even be a reality right now.

"Yeah?"

He nods. "Without a doubt. You're a natural. Not saying it will be easy, but think of it this way. You have a strong support system. You have me and Juliet, and Ari and Kennedy would love to meet him. Your mom. Your sister. You have people who wouldn't bat an eye if you called them for help. I don't know, man, no one can decide for you. It's scary and it's a lot thrown on you at once, but I know that you'll make the right decision."

I take another sip of my beer before nodding. After talking to Ma and Emery and now Liam... I feel like I have their support if I do decide to take Evan.

"I'm gonna do some soul searching tonight before I call her back. Things been okay with you and the girls?"

Liam smiles. "Well... I guess this is as good a time as any, seeing how my wife is bursting at the seams."

He picks up his phone and scrolls for a second then turns the phone toward me.

On the screen is a picture of... an ultrasound?

"Wait." I squint and lean forward to get a better look. "Is Juliet *pregnant?*"

Liam grins, and it lights up his entire face. "Holy shit! Congrats, man."

I leap from the chair, and he stands, hugging me. I slap my hand on his back in congratulations.

"Damn, daddy times three. How does it feel?"

He shakes his head. "Honestly? Fucking good, man. I'm happy. We weren't trying but not preventing either." He shrugs. "I can't wait to tell the girls. They're going to be so excited."

"Hope it's a boy?" I ask. Having two girls, he needs a guy in the house to be on his team every now and then.

"Yeah, but at the end of the day, I want a healthy baby and a healthy wife. That's all that matters."

I came over here for advice, and Liam gave it. Even if he didn't say anything out loud, the happiness and love that you feel when you step over the threshold and the genuine elation written on his face at the mention of his family, tells me everything I need to know.

My decision just became a whole lot easier.

CHAPTER FOUR
HOLLAND

I love books. Like, I *really* love them.

In fact, it's the reason I decided to become a librarian at only six years old. While most kids wanted to be superheroes, ballerinas and firefighters, I wanted to spend all day, every day locked inside a musty library, immersing myself in literature. Even as a child, my love for the written word surpassed everything else. I was never interested in barbies or dollhouses and definitely not dance classes. Reading and books became an escape for me. I lost myself in a different world every time I picked up a new book, living a thousand lives throughout their pages.

From the outside looking in, you'd think that my dream would be easy to obtain, but you'd be wrong. Dreams like that were only obtainable if you were born into a family that had the one thing I did not. Money.

No one really knew how badly we struggled growing up. I did my best to hide it where I could, and the only one who really knew the truth was Emery. My mother passed away when I was seven from breast cancer, and my dad basically fell apart. I was the glue that held it all together, even though I was only a child. My daddy worked long, grueling hours at the local paper mill for subpar pay and scarce benefits. But we made it...just barely.

The day I turned sixteen, I marched down Main Street to the library I had gone to since I was a child and practically begged for a job. It was the only place I could've imagined working. Thankfully, the librarian, Velma, had a soft spot for me and offered me part-time hours, and the rest is history.

I'm starting my first year of my Master's in Library Science at the University of Chicago... albeit online. My father got sick three years ago with dementia, so my days are spent here in the library, losing myself in the beauty of books, then caring for my father and going to class part-time at night.

My dream has taken longer than planned, but as my mother used to say... 'it's a journey, not a race.'

"Holland?"

My eyes dart up from the heavy book in my hands to see Velma staring at me with concern in her eyes.

"Are you okay?" she asks.

"Yes, I'm sorry. I was in another world." I apologize before sliding the book into its home on the shelf. I was so lost in thought I didn't even hear her approach.

"I'm closing up for the night, you're welcome to stay and study, of course, just please set the alarm and lock up when you leave."

She gives me a kind smile before leaving me with the cart of books I'm still putting away.

Some nights when Mona, my dad's nurse, sits with him, I stay at the library until late studying. Even though it technically isn't allowed, Velma gives me a free pass because she knows me so well.

My phone rings in my back pocket, and I pull it out and grin when I see Emery's picture on the screen.

"Please tell me you're calling me to let me know that you are *officially* done for fall break?"

Emery attends the University of Chicago and is currently in their Law program. She's the weird one who likes to binge serial-killer documentaries and podcasts on how to effectively dismember someone, but in real life is severely grossed out by blood and bodily fluids, so she chose law. 'At least she could be on the criminal justice side,' she says.

A low, sultry groan vibrates through the phone before she huffs. "One more exam, Hol, one more. I want to drown myself in cheap tequila and forget just how shitty these past few days have been."

"That's the understatement of the century." I scoff, pushing the book cart farther down the aisle, so I can talk and put away the rest of the books. "How are you? I mean... how are you *really*?"

Emery's quiet for a beat before she speaks, stopping me in my tracks.

"Em," I say her name softly, "talk to me. I'm here."

"I have been avoiding it. Honestly. He was a douche, and I knew he was, but it still doesn't make the sting any easier, ya know? Getting cheated on sucks."

"I know, but I think you're much better off. Your prince charming is going to ride in on his white horse and sweep you off your feet," I offer.

She sighs. "Just as long as he doesn't ride in on any type of sports equipment. Lord knows I have enough drama dealing with Reed and his posse."

Reed's name sets off a flurry of butterflies in my stomach.

Because I have a secret, one that *no one* knows. Especially not Emery. Because this secret? It would change *everything*.

The secret I've been holding in for so long is that I, Holland Parker, am ridiculously in love with Reed Davidson and I have been since I was nine years old, watching him save a kitten from a tree. It was one of those moments where I had hearts in my eyes, and after that, it seemed like whenever Reed was around, I couldn't stop the growing feeling deep in my stomach. Suddenly, he was no longer the boy next door or my best friend's older brother, but the boy who made my heart race a little faster when he was near.

Not that he knew how I felt. I never gave any inclination that I cared about him in any other way than the strictly platonic way. Reed was older, he was running in different crowds, so I spent every moment I could soaking up the little attention he graced to Emery and me.

I can't tell you how many nights I spent on the side of an ice rink, freezing to death, my nose so cold and red that I was sure I would get hypothermia... just to spend more time with him. It wasn't out of the ordinary because there was nowhere that Emery would've rather been than where Reed was.

Those two have a bond that a lot of people never get to experience in their lifetime. Being an only child, I've never had a bond so close, so tight knit, the way that they do. The closest thing I've ever had to a sister is Emery.

Which is why, under no circumstance, would I ever tell her about my childish crush on Reed. Not only would it change the dynamics of our friendship, but Emery and I made a promise to each other in the very beginning that as her best friend, I would *never, ever* (a middle schooler's promise, keep in mind) think of Reed as anything other than a brother.

She'd spent her entire middle school years being befriended by fake girls who wanted nothing but to get as close as they could to Reed. He had that effect on girls. He made them lovesick, and Emery was the casualty in a lot of those relationships gone bad.

But isn't that what girls do? Be friends with their new boyfriend's sister, only to drop her when they suddenly split?

I'd seen it time and time again, even after we became friends, hence the promise to each other.

Even though it was years ago, I never want to hurt Emery or be the reason that she feels betrayed, no matter how hopelessly in love with Reed I have been since middle school.

Breaking through my forbidden thoughts, she says, "So, I was thinking, do you want to go to this goat yoga class with me in the morning? Hella early, but whatever. I need it."

Wait. Goat... *yoga?*

"What the hell is goat yoga?" I laugh. During the conversation with Em, I've seemingly made my way through the cart of books and am finally down to the last one.

Em squeals. "Oh my god, listen, I saw it on Twitter and I knew that we had to do it. It's basically just yoga outdoors where you get to cuddle baby goats."

"Okay, that does sound amazing. I'm in. Hey, I totally forgot to ask. Do you think Reed has time to stop by to check the furnace? It's starting to get cooler at night and I swear it sounds like someone's in there banging it with a wrench every time it kicks on." I grimace. Seriously, I'm going to bang my own head against the furnace if it's on its way out. It's an expense that we truly can't afford right now. Not unless I can pick up more transcribing jobs on the side.

I've been picking up online transcribing jobs for a little extra cash when I'm not taking care of dad, working at the library or in class. So really, not many. But it's nice to have a little bit of money tucked away.

"Uh, so Reed is out of town for a bit for uh, some family stuff." Em stutters. "I'm sure he could look at it when he gets home."

"Yeah, maybe I'll just shoot him a text."

"Okay, well, I'll see you tomorrow morning. I'll text you the address. Love you, bye!"

She hangs up before I can even respond and I look down at my phone. Okay, well, that's settled. Goat yoga it is. I laugh to myself.

After the phone call with Em, I sit down at the large oak table, spread my books out and get to work. I only have one night off, tonight, so I have to get as much work done as possible.

Two nights later, I'm lying in bed, reading, when my phone buzzes. I'm so engrossed in the story that I don't bother to check the screen, thinking it must be a notification from social media, but then, seconds later... it rings again.

This time, I glance down at my phone and see Reed's name flashing on the screen.

Setting the book aside, I sit up quickly. Reed never calls me... like ever.

"Reed?" I whisper, careful not to wake my dad who's on the other side of the paper-thin wall.

"Uh, Holland, hey..." He trails off, and I hear a loud thump on the other end. "So, could you possibly come to my house? Like... now?"

"It's after midnight, everything okay?" I ask hesitantly. Even though I'm already getting out of bed, sliding my feet into my worn Vans, and grabbing my cardigan from the hanger on the back of my door.

"I'll explain when you get here. Okay?" He sounds like he's running a marathon.

"Okay, be there soon."

We hang up and I quietly tiptoe through the house, like I'm a teenager again, sneaking out. I lock the house up tight, and make sure Dad's sound asleep. He should be okay for a few minutes while I run to Reed's. He only lives a few minutes up the road from the house I share with my father. Except, he lives in the fancy part of town. I check my phone and verify that all of the indoor and outdoor cameras are working properly, and then I lock the deadbolt to the front door behind me.

My rusty, tin-can bucket of a car sits in the driveway. I've affectionately named her Betty. She's not much to look at on the outside, or well, the inside, but at least she has four wheels and gets me where I need to be. I've learned to appreciate the smaller things in life.

The entire ride to Reed's house, my mind is running a mile a minute. When I pull in the driveway and park, I notice that every single light in the house seems to be on.

Why is he calling after midnight? After our... weird moment at his house the other day, I wasn't expecting to see him again so soon. I'm surprised to say the least.

And... I'm nervous. This is the first time I've ever been to his house, alone. I take a few deep breaths to calm myself before I get out of the car and walk up the path to the front door. I raise my hand to knock, but before I can, the door swings open and Reed's standing on the other side.

I quickly drag my eyes up from his bare feet.

He's standing in front of me... shirtless. A pair of black gym shorts hang low on his hips, revealing the deep V that I can't seem to look away from. His dark mop of curls is a mess, like he's run his fingers through them a million times. Likely in frustration or anxiousness, just like he's always done. But what causes me to pause is the worried look in his dark, amber-flecked eyes. He's not his usual happy, playful self.

"Uh, hi?" I ask, my hand still suspended in midair.

"Come in." He opens the door wider for me to enter. When I pass him, I get the smallest whiff of his body wash, and I almost whimper.

God, Holland, how pathetic are you?

"So... What I'm about to tell you is highly confidential." He starts the second the front door is closed behind me.

I walk over to the bar stool, next to his kitchen island, set my purse down in front of me and slide onto the luxury wooded stool.

"Okaaaaay..."

"Seriously, Holl, it can't leave this room. It's important."

I roll my eyes. "You're as dramatic as Briggs, *what* is going on?"

Before he can answer me, a toddler, maybe two or three years old, comes padding down the hallway, clutching a worn octopus tightly to his little body.

"Daddy?"

"Oh my god," I whisper and grab onto the counter for dear life. I look back and forth between the tiny little boy, who has the same hair and dark eyes as the man standing in front of me, who looks as panicked as I feel.

The little boy's lower lip begins to tremble.

I look at Reed. "You have... a *child?*" I screech.

Holy. Shit.

This is a secret I don't think even *I* can keep.

CHAPTER FIVE
REED

Fuck, this is *not* going as planned.

I run my hand through my hair nervously and start pacing the kitchen. "Wait, no, I mean… sort of? I don't know, Holl." My words come out in a rush. "I'm his… guardian. He's mine now. This is Evan."

It feels like the strangest thing in the world to say. Just three days ago, I was at a bar with a bunny on my lap, talking about how sweet life is, and now my entire world's been turned upside down.

But I know it's nothing compared to what this little guy must be feeling.

Holland pulls her wide-eyed gaze from me and glances back at Evan, who looks like he's about two seconds from an absolute meltdown. I can't say I blame him; it's been the most exhausting two days of my life.

And I think this is what it's going to be like going forward. I'm trading in nights at the bar for nights on the couch, watching cartoons.

In the end, the decision was easy. I couldn't let my sister's child end up in foster care and be another child lost in the system. I couldn't abandon him. I *wouldn't.* He needs me.

After my discussion with Ma and Em, I booked the next flight to New York, called the team owner, Mark, and my coach, Rick, and let them know I'd have to miss practice for a few days because of everything going on. Thankfully, they understood and didn't give me any shit.

When the plane touched down in New York, I was more nervous than I could ever remember being in my life. Even more than my first game as an Avalanche. This was different. Once I met Evan, I knew life wouldn't ever be the same. How could it? How could I return to the life I knew before, knowing that there was this little boy out there who needed me?

It was more than just meeting my nephew for the first time in the shittiest of circumstances. I suddenly had the weight of the world on my shoulders. So many things riding on the fact that I was his new guardian.

My palms were clammy, my heart raced; it felt like my throat was going to close from how anxious I was. By the time I got into the cab to head to DCFS, I almost talked myself out of it at least twelve times. Walking through the front doors of that building, it felt like a douse of cold water straight to the face.

The reality of the situation hit me. That was it. I was going to meet my nephew for the first time and take him back home with him, and it would all happen within twenty-four hours.

Seeing him for the first time was nothing like I had tried to prepare myself for.

God, I wasn't prepared for him to look so... small.

Even though I had only met my half-sister a few times, I could see how much he looked like her. What was more shocking is how much he favored *me*. Dark hair, green eyes, dimples in his cheeks. Not that he offered me even a hint of a smile when I met him.

He looked up at me through teary eyes, clutching this old, ratty looking octopus that was missing an eye. I could see how sad he was, and fuck, it was like a punch to the gut. This poor kid. I can't even imagine going through what he has at such a young age.

He was probably scared out of his mind. I could feel the tremors in his hand as he took mine.

I knew right then I had made the right decision. I didn't feel an ounce of regret or hesitation. Seeing my nephew solidified that there was never really even a question. We hadn't spoken a word and I felt this protectiveness over him that I couldn't explain. Maybe because I see so much of myself in him, and don't want him to go through the same things that I did.

Connie, the social worker, took over shortly after, getting everything organized for Evan to come with me, and it was a flurry of paperwork. I signed so much shit my hand almost fell off, all while Evan sat quietly beside me in an old metal chair. The entire process felt entirely transactional; just sign here on the dotted line and now you suddenly have a child to care for. A signature and a stamp. I suddenly felt even more for the children that had no choice but to be placed in the foster care system.

We did my background check and fingerprints, and she said someone from my state would be coming by in the next twelve hours for an emergency home check, and that was that.

I was officially the guardian of a three-year-old little boy whose parents had just been killed.

Just. Like. That.

We checked into a five-star resort hotel near Times Square, and as soon as we walked into the room and he laid on the bed, he was out.

Not me. I'm pretty sure I didn't sleep a wink the entire night. Instead, I watched him sleep to make sure he was... you know, breathing. Fuck, I didn't know. I was new at this and scared I was going to screw it all up.

He hadn't said more than a few words to me besides juice, food... shit like that. And thankfully, I knew how to change a diaper from Ari and Ken, or I would've really been fucked. We flew the short distance home with his clammy palm tightly grasping mine.

The entire thing was so damn surreal.

It's been twenty-four hours, and we're making it. He's timid around me, which is to be expected, and I'm doing the best I can. Except tonight, he's been waking up with what I'm guessing are night terrors because he falls asleep, only to wake up screaming. We're both exhausted, but I can't figure out what to do. Ma and Em both didn't answer the seventeen times I called them, but go figure, the time I seriously need help. Then, Liam didn't answer, and I was freaking out. So... I called Holland. The only other person I trust who might actually have an idea of what to do.

"Reed..." Holland says warily. She hops down from the stool and slowly approaches Evan. Judging by his death grip on the octopus, he's having a rough time.

"My sister... Amelia. My half-sister. She and her husband were killed in a robbery gone wrong in New York. Robert has cancer and can't care for him, so... I was the next in line for guardianship. It was either I take him in or he goes into foster care. Holland, I couldn't let the kid become a ward of the state." I lower my voice and curse. "Shit, I don't know what I'm doing. The very limited things I do know are not enough to be a... single parent."

The words feel foreign on my tongue.

Holland's wary eyes soften into something different. A flicker of sympathy. She sits down in front of Evan, her long blonde hair swaying as she does. "Hi Evan. My name is Holland. Is that your octopus?" She nods at the plush animal in his arms.

Evan looks down and back at Holland then nods slightly.

"I love it." She smiles widely. "What's its name?"

"Pickles."

I let out a low laugh, and Evan hits me with a death stare, so I drop it immediately.

Shit. This kid is a tough crowd.

"You know when I was your age, I used to have a stuffed monkey named Arthur that I carried everywhere. He made me feel so brave. I was *never* afraid when he was around."

43

Evan drags his eyes up to hers and sniffles. His little feet shuffle from side to side while he rubs his already red-rimmed, puffy tear-filled eyes with the other hand.

"I think he's having nightmares... I tried to calm him down but he just... He's not having it. I didn't know what to do," I say quietly. Holland nods her head.

"Evan, what if we put on a cartoon and just hang out for a while with Pickles? Is that okay?"

She extends her hand for him to hold and he looks down at it, obviously trying to decide if she's a safe bet or not, then finally slides his tiny hand in hers.

I exhale with relief.

The two of them walk over to the couch, and then I hand Holland the remote. She puts on something about a baby shark that has way too much music for me, but Evan finally relaxes into the couch. For the first time since he walked in, it seems like he's... Okay.

This can't be easy for him; I can't imagine how much he misses his parents, even though he probably doesn't fully grasp what is happening.

I walk over and stand by the bar and check my email, responding to a few endorsements that I have pending, and shoot my coach and the owner each a message with an update. I need to get back to practice, but I can't leave him.

Not after everything he's been through in the past few days.

My eyes drift back to Holland; she's pulling the blanket up

Evan's chest and gingerly lifting herself from the couch. He's still holding her hand and it causes this weird feeling in my chest.

Shit, I'm so in over my head.

Carefully unwinding his tight grasp, she places his tiny hand back on his chest and stands, walking over to where I'm standing by the island. "Wow." She breathes as she slides back onto her spot on the bar stool. "I can honestly say this was the last thing I expected when you called."

"Yeah, it happened so quickly, I barely had time to process it. Hell, I'm still in shock. Then he was crying in his sleep and I just... I tried to call Em and Ma, but apparently, they sleep like the dead."

Holland nods. "I think Em was taking some sleeping medicine earlier. With everything going on, she said she was going to go to bed early tonight and try and catch up on sleep. Exams just finished."

"I'm scared I'm going to fuck this up," I mutter.

"Kids are resilient, Reed. You'd be surprised. I'm sure he misses his parents and the change will be hard for him, but you'll be amazing. I know it. I understand it's probably scary and overwhelming to be in your shoes right now, but I have no doubt that it'll work out exactly the way that it should."

I wasn't confident in that, not in the least, but fuck knows I'll try and be everything I can for him. For Holland to have this much faith in me... it feels like the best compliment in the world.

"I think we just need to get to know each other. Right now, we're strangers. He doesn't even know me and I've taken him from the only home he does know."

Her brows furrow and she's quiet for a moment, thinking things over. "You know what might help? Making a space that's his. Like, doing a room where he feels comfortable and at ease in his new environment. Maybe talk with the social worker and see what his room was like back home? And try to make a similar version here."

Shit, that is a good idea. "You are a godsend, Holland."

A pink blush floods her cheeks, and she rolls her eyes. "I took a course on child development as an elective, at least I learned a little to apply to real life."

"Well, it shows. You're great with him."

It's comments like that and her unwavering confidence in me that make it even more difficult to stop thinking about her. Honestly, ever since the other night when I picked her and Em up at the sorority house, I haven't been able to stop thinking about her.

Just like now, the way she's standing in front of me, shyly fidgeting with the buttons on her cardigan, she's beautiful. Effortlessly so.

My hands itch to run down the ample curves of her hips. Holland isn't rail thin by any means, and I know from having her at my house twenty-four-seven since we were kids, she's always been self-conscious about her weight.

When she was a freshman, I broke a kid's nose because he called her a cow. There was nothing remotely unattractive about her body. Not in the slightest. She's a fucking knockout, and I guess I never allowed myself a second glance at her since she's Emery's best friend, but now, I can't seem to stop looking at her.

She's wearing a pair of yoga pants that flare at her hips and hug her ample curves. I'm captivated, and I need to get my head on straight.

"Reed?"

My eyes drag up to hers, and she's looking at me curiously.

Busted.

"Yeah?"

"I asked if you thought of a plan yet? Where's Evan going to go to school?"

The thoughts that I most definitely should not be having are all but vanished by her question.

"Fuck," I pause, dragging my hands through my hair and down my face and beard, "I don't know what I'm going to do, Holland. Hockey is my job. I have to get back on the ice, but I can't leave him here while I'm on the road for six months out of the year. The kid's been through hell and back. He's probably traumatized at this point. Imagine someone new, someone different, yet again, coming in and throwing his world out of whack. I need to build a relationship with him, bond with him. It's the most important thing." I walk over to the fridge and pull a water out for each of us then set one in front of her. "I wish there was a handbook for this shit. An easy manual that told me exactly what to do."

"I'm pretty sure every parent wishes for that. I think that you have an awesome support system, and you do know kids. Even if it's not raising one full-time by yourself, you have lots of practice with Ari and Kennedy."

I nod. Fuck, she's right. It just doesn't feel that way right now. It feels overwhelming and exhausting, and like every move I make is going to be the wrong one.

Holland reaches out and places her hand over mine on the bar. "Don't be so hard on yourself. Trust your gut."

Her phone vibrates and she pulls it from her purse and mutters a curse. "I'm sorry, Reed, I have to go. I think my Dad's up. The camera is going off."

"Go, you've done more than enough here. Thank you. For tonight."

"You don't have to thank me, Reed. He just... he needs someone to love him right now. He might not fully understand what's happening, but he knows that he's had to leave his home and that he hasn't seen his parents. It's just going to be a lot of learning and a lot of healing. For both of you." She hops down from the stool and grabs her purse, throwing it over her shoulder.

"Be careful. I'm gonna come by tomorrow and look at the furnace. I talked to Em and she mentioned that you were having trouble with it. Her and Ma want to take Evan to get some clothes and spend time with him, so I'll have a few free hours to stop by."

"No, Reed, you have too much going on. It's okay. I can call a handyman."

"I'm coming by. It's the least I can do. I'll see you tomorrow, kay?"

I walk her to the door and she walks out as soon as I open it.

"Bye Reed."

Her light, ocean-colored eyes shine in the pale glow of night, and she gives me a shy smile before waving and getting into her car.

When I brought Evan home tonight, I didn't know what to expect. Hell, I still don't. But after the conversation with Holland and hearing her confidence in me, I feel like I can handle this. It won't be easy, but I've never been someone to give up when things get hard.

It's the one thing I learned from the man who *didn't* raise me.

CHAPTER SIX
HOLLAND

It's been less than twenty-four hours since I've seen Reed and still, my stomach flutters and dips when I hear the doorbell ring.

Every time I catch myself thinking of him, a twist of guilt forms in the pit of my stomach. Not just because I feel like I'm betraying Emery, but because I feel selfish in allowing myself to feel this way about him, even if it is in secret.

I don't want to jeopardize my relationship with Em, so therefore, the secret crush on Reed I've been harboring will remain just that. A secret.

Dad looks up from his recliner in the living room when I pass by to get the door. He gives me a small smile, and I remember why it is that I work so hard. For him.

I open the door, and Reed's there smiling, charming and bright. He's casual today in jeans, a worn white tee and sneakers that look like he's had them for a decade. It reminds me of the days when we were younger and he was always outside on the ice, playing hockey with his friends.

"Morning," he says.

"Good morning." I swing the door open wider, gesturing for him to come inside.

When he steps into the foyer, he looks around. "Wow, this place hasn't changed at all since we were kids."

"Yeah, I try to keep things familiar for Dad."

He nods, understanding what I'm saying without having to say it. Dad's dementia has taken a turn in the last few years, and each day that I have him, really have him, is a day I cherish.

Reed may be on the road six months out of the year, but he and my dad have always had a friendly relationship. We've lived next door to the Davidsons for over half my life. Whenever their lawnmower broke and Reed was kicking and cursing the thing after trying to get it working again, my dad went over and helped. When Dad needed help painting the garage, Reed spent the entire day painting with him and never once complained or expected anything in return. Anytime Dad needed help with the boat that dad adored, when we were younger, Reed would come over and spend the day in the shop working on it with him.

Reed walks into the living room and his face softens when he sees Dad in the recliner. "Hey, old man."

Dad looks up and his eyes light up the second he sees Reed. He's having a good morning; he must recognize him.

"Ah, you're a hot shot hockey player now. Think you're too good to come around and visit this old man anymore?"

Dad tries to stand from the recliner, but his legs are shaky and he's having trouble. Reed immediately steps in and offers him his arm. He lifts him from the chair effortlessly, so Dad can stand face to face with him, and shake his hand.

The entire thing causes tears to well in my eyes, and I quickly swipe them away. I don't want Reed to see. It just... does something to my heart to see him treat my dad with so much respect and love. It makes my heart ache in the same way because my dad is losing himself more and more every day, and there is nothing I can do to stop it. Nothing that I can do to lessen the pain of his life fading. To help him be the person he's always been and not feel like less of a man. I can hardly stand the pain in my chest on his bad days.

The days that he forgets me or calls me by my mother's name. It's difficult, and it's even harder knowing that I'm helpless, that I have to sit back and watch it happen without being able to change it.

"Nah, never. You know how much I enjoy sharing a beer. I came by to fix the furnace, it's been acting up for Holland."

"That damn thing, it's as old as she is. I've been meaning to replace it, but I've been real busy at the Mill."

I still. *Oh Daddy.*

Reed doesn't skip a beat; he just pats dad on the back. "You take care of yourself, okay? Come on over to Ma's if you need any help with the boat, alright?"

Dad smiles and shakes his hand again.

"Don't be a stranger, you here? I miss ya, kid."

Only then do I let the tears fall hot and heavy down my cheeks; I leave the foyer and walk into the kitchen to have a moment to compose myself. I didn't imagine a situation like this when Reed said he was coming to fix the furnace, and I am not emotionally prepared for it.

"Holland?" Reed's voice, deep and husky, comes from the entryway of the kitchen, and I swipe away a few stray tears and turn toward him, giving him a watery smile.

"Sorry, I'm just-" He cuts me off and stalks over, pulling me into his arms.

It takes me off guard. The comfort, the closeness, all of it. I grew up with Reed, but it's not like we've spent much time touching each other. It's exactly what I needed in this moment but would've never asked for.

I squeeze my eyes shut and bite my lip until I taste the metallic tinge of blood as I attempt to hold back a sea of tears. Reed's hand strokes the back of my head as I let out a small whimper.

"Don't apologize for feeling, Holland. I know it's hard, and you do it all by yourself."

I nod against his embrace.

"Thank you." I pull back and look at him.

His lips tug up in a small grin as he releases me. "You're right, though, it's cold as shit in here. Why in the hell didn't you call someone sooner?"

I shrug, and start walking toward the basement. Reed follows closely behind, so close I can feel the heat radiating from his body.

I guess I've gotten used to the cold without realizing it.

"It's not that cold."

Except every step we take down into the basement, the colder it gets. By the time we've gotten to the last one, I can see my breath in front of me.

Maybe it's a tad bit colder than I realized.

"Holland," Reed says sternly, shaking his head.

"What? I've been using space heaters in the house."

He brushes past me toward the furnace, grabbing Dad's tool bag that's on the table. He shakes his head once more before he lowers himself beneath the furnace and starts working. I take the opportunity to hop onto the table and watch.

Every time he lifts the wrench, his white shirt pulls up slightly and shows the light scatter of hair above the waistband of his jeans.

Ugh. Out of all people to be obsessed with, why does it have to be my best friend's brother? The one person in the world I can't ever have.

After a few minutes of clanking and cursing, Reed sits up. The furnace is on now, but making god-awful noises. The wooden shelf above Reed vibrates every time the machine groans.

"This thing is fucked. And even if it didn't sound so damn horrible, I don't think it would even pass inspection." Just as he says the words, the furnace grumbles and sputters, getting increasingly louder by the second.

"Uh, I think we might need to turn it off, Reed."

Before he can get off the floor, the shelf above the furnace, that is full to the brim with books that didn't fit on my shelves upstairs, cracks, and almost in slow motion, it falls on top of Reed.

"Oh my god," I yell, hopping down from my perch on the table.

"Oof." Reed groans, pulling books off his face. "Goddamnit."

I make it over to him and start to pull the old, worn books off of him until I can see his face, and make sure he's not actually injured. "Holy shit, are you okay?" I screech, panicking.

My hands feel all over him to make sure there isn't anything broken or any sign of visible trauma. They slide down the hard planes of his pecs, down his rock-hard abs, and even down his thighs.

Great, that's all I need. To injure the best center in the entire NHL and have the sports world hate me for being responsible. It's also impossible not to freak out that my hands are on him; I mean, he could be injured and I'm over here thinking about how hard his muscles are.

"Holland." He groans again, only this time, it sounds deeper, raspier. His eyes are squeezed shut tightly, and his breathing is labored.

"Did you break your leg, or your hands? Oh god, can you still walk?" I cry. My hands travel up and down his body again, feeling for any type of injury. I find nothing but hard, unwavering muscle.

"Stop."

I freeze, immediately.

Reed sits up on his elbows and looks down at me. "I'm not

going to be okay if you keep touching me."

Holy shit. My eyes dart down to where he's adjusting himself then back up to his face. Oh god, Reed was getting turned on from *my* hands being on him. *Jesus, Holland, your hands are practically on his dick.*

I snatch them away quickly and mumble, "I'm sorry."

Except I'm not, *at all.* Well, maybe a little, because now I'm embarrassed. My cheeks are burning.

"I'm pretty sure that your precious *Pride and Prejudice* missed my dick by half a centimeter." He lifts the book that was lying on his stomach.

With that, I throw my head back and let out a loud, completely ungraceful laugh that includes snorting and tears. I collapse on my knees to the side, clutching my stomach, thinking about Reed Davidson being injured by a classic novel.

"Oh god, that is the funniest thing I've ever heard." I rasp.

"Yeah? You think it's funny that I almost lost my dick to a book, Holland?" There's playfulness in his tone, but his words have the opposite effect. And that's when I realize just how close we are. Somewhere in the shuffle, we've come so close together that I can feel how harshly he's breathing, whether it's from the falling shelf or that he's feeling the same thing I am, I don't know.

His deep brown eyes gaze into mine, and I suddenly feel exposed. Open. Raw.

On display for Reed Davidson.

"Holland." He whispers my name raggedly, and for the first

time, I think he might feel the same way that I do. I can hear the tortured tone of his voice. The same hesitation that I feel, but wish wasn't present; the same way that I want him to kiss me, but he knows he can't.

That we can't.

I tuck a loose piece of hair behind my ear and look away, the intensity of his stare burning directly to my core.

"Fuck, you're beautiful."

My heart begins to race in my chest, unsure of what's happening, but too selfish to stop it. His words cause me to shiver, a delicious fire that seems to start in my stomach and burn all the way to the sensitive spot between my thighs.

He leans closer, and I don't pull away. I simply suck in a gasp.

Ring, Ring, Ring

His phone sounds, causing us both to jump, and the spell we were just under to be broken.

"Shit." He clears his throat then curses before pulling it out of his pocket then swiping and answering. I busy myself by picking up the books around him while he talks.

"Hey Ma. Yeah, finishing up here and then I'll be on my way. I know. Yes. Yes. Ma... yes."

He ends the call and puts it back into his pocket. Just as quickly as the conversation starts, it's over, leaving us both in a tense, uncharted silence.

What happens now?

"You need a new furnace, Holl. This shit is not safe, and you can't run it. Someone would need to come out, inspect the gas lines, make sure everything is working properly, not to mention replace the damn furnace."

"I- we... It's just not possible right now, Reed," I whisper, feeling my cheeks aflame from embarrassment.

I hate the raw vulnerability I feel about exposing how bad our money situation is. It's embarrassing. But, it's the truth. The simple answer is we can't afford thousands of dollars on a furnace, and insurance is not going to cover manual wear and tear. We've needed to replace it for a while, but never had the funds to do so.

"What's wrong? Is everything okay?"

I look away, unable to meet his stare. "We can't afford it. I have savings, but it's not nearly enough. We'll just have to make do."

"I'll pay for it all."

Whipping my head back to him my jaw drops. What?

He obviously got knocked in the head when the shelf fell. That's the only reason he'd say something so ludicrous.

"Absolutely not. I'll take care of it. The space heaters will be fine for now."

"Holland, I have the money. I have plenty of it. I won't be able to sleep at night knowing you're alone in this freezing-ass house." He shakes his head. "Just please, let me do this."

"No." I shake my head vehemently, and stand from the cold floor. "I told you I would handle it and I will. I'll pick up a few more shifts at the library when I'm not doing my online classes."

Reed stands abruptly and looks at me. He runs his hand

through his beard before he starts to pace back and forth on the basement floor. "Listen... I have an idea. It might be fucking crazy, but I think- I think that it would work."

"Okay."

"What if... what if you came on the road with me? Just hear me out," he pauses, holding his hands up, "just to keep an eye on Evan while I'm at practice or have a game. I will get you tickets for every game, so you'd really just have to bring him."

"That is crazy, Reed. Don't make something insane up just to buy me a new furnace. I can fig-"

He cuts me off. "Just listen. I'm not making it up and it benefits me too. I'm saying this selfishly. I'll pay you a salary. A ridiculously large one. And before you say anything, you'd be helping me out more than you know, Holland. I can't just leave him with a stranger that I don't know, and I'm not even entertaining the idea of leaving him behind. Your classes are online... so it wouldn't interfere, right?"

It wouldn't... but... I can't just go with Reed. On the road. For an entire hockey season.

Could I?

"Just think about it. This way, you can make a decent amount of money, save up, and it would be saving my ass tenfold. It's only during practice and games, and I'll book you a room. I know your dad has Mona, but I'll pay for a night nurse too. The absolute best care money can buy."

Dad's nurse, Mona, would probably be okay staying with him

on the days that I would be gone.

"And put all of that aside, okay. Look, Evan just met you and he already likes you, hell, probably more than me. He obviously trusts you, and is comfortable with you and... right now? That's everything to him. And to me. It's not just me that needs you... it's Evan too."

Oh God, am I seriously considering this? He's tugging directly on the strings of my heart by mentioning Evan and the fact that he needs me.

Reed's right, though, about all of it. I need to be able to fix this stupid furnace and all of the other things that are falling apart around here, and not to mention, save up for the next emergency, so I don't have to stress about it.

"This is a terrible idea," I mutter.

He steps closer to me, not quite touching, but almost. "Please, Holland. This is me, Reed Davidson, the hottest hockey star you'll ever meet, begging you. I need you. I promise it'll be worth your while. This solves my problems, and yours. What could it hurt? Just... give me the hockey season. That's all I need, and then I'll find someone else. Six months."

When he puts it like that...He's right.

What did I have to lose?

"Deal."

The words are out of my mouth before I can talk myself out of it.

CHAPTER SEVEN
REED

"That was a cheap fucking shot, asshole." I grunt, using the back of my glove to wipe away the sweat on my brow.

"Pass the damn puck then." Ledger grins.

Fuck, it feels good to be back on the ice. The one place where I seem to not fuck anything up. When my blade hits the ice, it's like everything fades away. I feel on top of the goddamn world, and it's a feeling that I'll never stop chasing. The high that hockey gives me.

The past few days have been a whirlwind, and I still can't believe Holland is going to come on the road with me. Or the almost kiss that happened. Was it a little crazy? Yeah. Is it probably a bad idea to be in such close proximity with the girl who is suddenly making my dick hard just by opening her mouth... absofuckinglutely, but it's done.

I couldn't leave Evan home with a stranger, and I wasn't even going to entertain the idea. Not after Holland agreed to help me out. Maybe next year, when he's more comfortable with me in general.

Shit's rocky. He's hesitant around me, and still trying to

understand what's happening, but I'm doing the best I can. Neither of us know what we're doing, but somehow... we're doing it together.

"Davidson, you gonna play fucking hockey or you going to daydream?" Coach bellows, pulling me from my thoughts.

Shit. I gotta get my head out of my ass. I skate back toward the center, and flick the puck around the end of my stick.

The rest of practice flies by. Being center for the best hockey team in the country means that this is my fucking show. There's no room for fucking off or mistakes. It's my job to score, and to make sure that we take home the cup this year. Hockey is my life, and even though my world's just been flipped upside down, it's my constant. Just like it's always been.

I step off the ice and rip my gloves off, tossing them on the bench in the box.

We're leaving tomorrow and that means that the next three days will be spent with Evan and Holland. I booked a separate room for Holland and a suite, so Evan would have his own space, but fuck, I'm nervous about being alone... with Holland. Because I want to be alone with Holland, and the things I want to do with her are things that can never happen.

"What's up with you tonight?" Hudson asks. He's our goalie, and one of my best friends. Most of us get along pretty well, but I'm closest to Graham, Briggs, Hudson, and Asher. Minus Liam, but he's coaching for a high school team now, so I don't get to see him as much as I did when he was coaching the Avalanche.

Briggs walks out of the showers with a towel around his hips. "Your head wasn't there tonight. Surprised Coach didn't make you run drills."

"Fucking got so much shit going on," I say as I pull a fresh t-shirt from my bag. "You know Holland? Emery's friend. The one who's lived next to Ma since we were kids?"

Briggs nods.

"I asked her to come on the road and help out with Evan during games and practice."

"Okay, and?"

I pause, raking my hands through my hair. "I just never really noticed her until recently. Like really fucking noticed her. She's gorgeous and I don't trust my dick when it's in the same vicinity as her."

I feel guilty for even thinking about it, let alone being this affected by her.

"Dude, Emery would literally break your limbs. She's weird like that. That's your little sister's best friend, if there was ever someone who was off-limits to you, it's her. Don't go there," Graham mutters. "I don't even know Emery that well and I know she's four-foot-eleven of pure violence." He shudders.

Slamming my locker shut, I hoist my bag up onto my shoulder and grab my stick. "I'm not. The fucking problem is that I know that, but my dick hasn't gotten the memo..." I trail off.

"She's just... I don't know, different. I know I shouldn't, I fucking know, but it doesn't mean that I'm not."

"You know that Em will cut your dick off."

He's right. Emery would lose her mind if she thought there was anything suspicious going on between Holland and me. Not that there is, but I've seen how Holland blushes profusely when I've teased her, or she leans in the smallest amount whenever I'm close. After the other day at her house, in the basement when I almost gave in and kissed the fuck out of her, the last thing I need to do is put myself in the position of being alone with her.

This is a bad idea. I know it, Briggs knows it, hell, anyone who knows my sister and the tiny terror that she is... knows it.

Not like my life wasn't already a total shitshow and as complicated as it could possibly be, inheriting my dead sister's kid, whom I've never met and who wants absolutely nothing to do with me. Let's throw in having the hots for my sister's best friend.

I groan and look up at the ceiling. "I'm completely fucked."

After practice, I head home and walk in the door just after nine. Tonight was particularly grueling, since I took a few days off to be with Evan. As soon as I shut the door behind me, Emery bounces into the entryway, way too fucking hyper.

"Holy shit." I laugh, grabbing the wall to keep upright.

"Me and Evan had a Nerf gun war. It was *amazing*." She squeals. She's grinning from ear to ear, and I'd be lying if I said I wasn't happy as fuck to see her so happy. It's been a long time since I've seen my sister smile like this. And the fact that it's Evan who's making her smile?

Icing on the cake.

I grin and toss my bag on the floor and kick off my shoes. "Bet he whipped your ass, huh?"

Her eyes roll and she prances over to the couch where she flops back down. "I let him win. It was so much fun, Reed. Seriously, I had a blast. He laughed so much."

"He's a great kid. I hate that he's going through so much. I can't imagine losing Ma."

Emery nods.

"I heard about Holl coming on the road with you. You better not be a dick to her." Her expression is stone, and I almost laugh.

Emery's pint-sized, five years younger, and weighs a third of what I do, but if I'm honest, my baby sister is a ball-buster, and she won't hesitate to beat my ass, especially when it comes to her best friend. She crosses her arms over her chest and narrows her eyes at me.

My eyes narrow, offended. "I am the nicest brother you have, Emery."

A throw pillow comes flying at my face.

"You're the only brother I have, dipshit. I'm serious. No weird Reed shit, and be a gentleman."

"Why the third-degree, Em? We're helping each other out. Don't make it something it isn't."

Even as I say it, the words feel bitter on my tongue. The truth is, I want Holland and I wish there wasn't every obstacle in the damn world standing in my way.

Emery stands from the couch and walks over to me. "Reed,

she's the most important person in my life. I just don't want something to happen and for me to lose her. All I have is you, mom and Holland."

Guilt sets in.

"Look, baby sis, everything's fine. No need to worry. I'll be on my best behavior. Now, I have to be up at the ass crack of dawn to head out. Text me when you make it home? And don't forget."

She looks like she has more to say, but nods and grabs her purse from the side table.

"Love you, dickhead."

"Love you, brat."

The front door shuts quietly behind her; seconds later, I hear the sound of her engine starting then her driving away.

Things are about to get even more complicated, but what's life without a little complication?

Or at least that's what I keep telling myself.

CHAPTER EIGHT
REED

"Wow, this is incredible." Holland breathes as she takes in Boston. It is gorgeous at night, especially downtown, but the beauty that I'm looking at has nothing to do with the city. "I've never been out of Chicago."

Her admission surprises me. The city lights seem to shine in her eyes, and the entire ride she barely glances away from the view.

"Really?" I ask. We're sitting in the back seat of an Uber, just having gotten off the plane and heading to our hotel that's close to the arena. It's our first night on the road together, and Evan hasn't been able to sit still the entire night.

"Car, fast! Fast," he cries. The loudest I've ever heard him speak since he's come to live with me. It's the first time I've seen him come out of his shell and call me a pussy, but it causes my heart to squeeze.

"Car is fast, buddy," I tell Evan.

Holland ruffles his hair before she speaks, "We never really had the money to travel. Plus, I've been working and studying from sun up to sun down since I was like sixteen." She laughs, trying to brush off what she's said, but I feel like a total asshole. I never realized that Holland and her dad had it so rough. Sure, she was at my house, more than she wasn't, growing up, but I figured it was because she and Em were attached at the hip, but the past few days have revealed a lot about Holland that I didn't know... or didn't pay attention to, at least.

I feel like a total dick for not noticing these things about her.

"We don't fly home till tomorrow night, maybe we can go sightseeing tomorrow?"

She nods. "I'd love that."

"We don't always have downtime before or after a game. It just so happened to work like that this time. We could see Fenway Park? Or maybe the Boston Public Library? I know how you are about books."

Her face lights up. "I would love to, but I don't think Evan would find that very much fun."

True. He probably wouldn't be able to sit still but... there are plenty of things to see in Boston.

"We'll figure out something to do."

A few minutes later, the Uber is pulling up to the curb outside the hotel, and we all get out.

"I'll grab the luggage. I only packed a bag for me and Evan."

Holland looks a bit guilty before she says, "I may have overpacked... a small amount."

I raise my eyebrows and when the driver pops the trunk and I see her massive suitcase, that's at least three of Evan, I groan in mock annoyance. "You sure you packed enough stuff for two days?"

She shrugs. "I didn't know what I would need, so I packed it all. I'm an overpacker."

"Ya think?" I lift the ridiculously heavy suitcase from the trunk and grab my duffle bag, then we head inside the hotel to check in. The concierge is polite and quick about situating the rooms and soon, we've got our keys in hand, and are headed toward the elevator.

"Sir, I'm so sorry for the inconvenience, but we're currently servicing the elevator. If you come right this way, the staircase is available."

You've got to be shitting me. I've got to lug this two-hundred-pound suitcase up three flights of stairs?

I smile at Evan, who's holding onto Holland's hand tightly, and Holland looks at me with a grimace. "Sorry," she mouths.

"Ladies first." I gesture toward the stairs.

The first two flights are fine. I'm a fucking hockey player, I fight guys that weigh three hundred pounds. It would have remained fine if the wheel of the damn suitcase didn't get stuck on the landing of our floor, making me tug a little harder than necessary, and causing the entire goddamn thing to fly open, spilling clothes, shoes and toiletries all over the floor.

"Shit. I'm sorry, Holland."

Holland laughs, brushing it off, and bends down to help me put everything back inside. Evan giggles as he watches us pick everything up.

Got it easy, little man. You get to stand there and look adorable while I lug this thing up the stairs.

I'm scooping things up until I pick up a red, sheer scrap of lace. I freeze, my brain going completely blank the second I realize what it is.

Did Holland pack... *lingerie?* Or is this what she always wears underneath her modest sweaters and ripped jeans?

My mouth goes dry. I swallow thickly, trying to gain back rational thought, but it escapes me. When Holland realizes what I've got in my hand, her cheeks flame the same color of her nightie and she snatches it from my hand and shoves it back into the half-opened suitcase.

Fuck. Fuck. Fuck.

Now I can't stop picturing her wearing nothing but that little red negligee, and me ripping it off of her into a pile of tattered lace on the floor. I want it, fuck, I *need* it.

"Weed?" Evan asks, breaking my trance. He pronounces his r's like w's, so he's taken to calling me, weed. Honestly, I don't even give a shit. At least he's opening up to me.

I clear my throat, swallowing down the thoughts in my head. "Sorry, buddy. You hungry?"

Evan nods. For a three-year-old kid that's been through the shit he has, he's a great kid. He's quiet. Observant, for a toddler, and can even play by himself.

Holland quickly picks up her clothes that have fallen out, and I hand her the card to her room. She's obviously embarrassed and is avoiding my eyes, but fuck, I can't stop picturing her in it.

We make it to our rooms as she shifts nervously from one foot to the other. "So, tomorrow?

I nod. "Yeah, uh, meet here in the morning? Eight?"

She nods. "Okay. Goodnight, Evan." She leans down and gives him a hug then faces me. "Goodnight, Reed."

"Goodnight."

I bring Evan into our room, and for the rest of the night, my thoughts are consumed with Holland Parker.

"What's on the agenda for today? You decide," I ask Holland as we walk out of the hotel toward the closest subway station. Evan's hand is clasped tightly in mine, and everything we pass, he wants to stop and admire. Can't say that I blame him. At his age, everything's big and exciting and I like seeing the world through his eyes.

Holland's eyes are just as wide and full of wonder as she takes in the city. I can't believe she's never been outside of Chicago before. At least now that she's traveling with us, she can see new places and experience new things.

"That's a lot of pressure, Reed," she mutters, chewing on her lip.

I chuckle. "Not really. Pick what you wanna do, and me and Ev are down for the ride. Anything."

"Anything?" she asks.

"Within reason."

She hits me playfully on the shoulder. "I mean, we could go to Fenway. I could be a baseball fan."

My eyes narrow and I shake my head. "I'm going to pretend you didn't just say that."

The audacity of this girl.

"I'm kidding, I'm kidding." Holland pulls out her phone as we walk and starts typing away furiously. "Oh, what about this?" She shows me her screen.

"Boston Tea Party ship and museum? That sounds awesome. I think Evan would love it."

She nods. "I've never even been on a boat, and this is like a giant replica of a historic one. We have to go. It looks like we catch the Blueline over there."

"You have ridden the subway before, right?" I tease. She lives in Chicago, so I know she has, but I like getting a rise out of her.

She rolls her eyes and looks back down at the subway map on her phone. "Yes, I've ridden the subway. I just haven't ever seen outside of Chicago. I've always wanted to, though."

We walk the rest of the way in comfortable silence, aside from Evan's excited chatter. Who knew a three-year-old could have so much to say? A short subway ride and walk later, and we've made it to the boat.

Holy shit, they weren't kidding, this thing is a legit replica.

Well, if I had to guess what the Boston Tea Party ship looked like.

Evan gasps when he sees it. "A pirate ship, Weed?" He's so excited he's bouncing on his toes, clutching Pickles.

Not gonna lie, there aren't many things better than seeing the genuine excitement on his face and I never realized how much I needed his happiness until now.

I knew I was unprepared when I made the decision to be his guardian; hell, it was one of the things I struggled with, the idea of fucking it up. I'm still scared to death, and man enough to admit it. Seeing him smiling and happy, though, thriving despite the situation he's been thrown into, makes it all worth it.

We are taking it one day at a time.

"Yes, bud, it's a ship. Do you wanna go on it?"

Evan nods enthusiastically, and Holland grins then holds out her hand. He slides his hand in hers, and we walk over to the ticket line.

After a few minutes wait, we're walking across the breezeway, boarding the ship. The wind causes the boat to rock gently, and Evan freezes. I can feel how still he becomes when the wood under our feet shifts slightly.

He immediately erupts into tears, and grabs onto my leg for dear life.

"Buddy, it's okay. It's okay," I say, trying to soothe him.

It only seems to make him cry harder. His grip on my leg is surprisingly tight for a toddler and I wince as he inches higher and higher, practically climbing my leg.

Holland doesn't even blink, she kneels down beside us both and gets on Evan's level. She places a soothing hand on his back and rubs gently. "Evan, it's okay. You're safe. Remember how brave Pickles makes you?"

He sniffles but buries his head into my jeans and stays silent. She looks up and gives me a small smile, reassuring me that it's going to be okay. I'm as panicked as he is. That's the thing about becoming Evan's guardian, I don't have all the answers. I don't know how to expertly diffuse any given situation. I don't know a lot of things, and every day that passes I learn new things. About both him and me. Parenting doesn't come with a handbook, even though I wish like fuck it did, but isn't that what makes you a good one, the fact that you learn from every situation thrown your way? You take your mistakes and learn from them?

That's all I can hope for. To be the kind of parent that my father never was.

I pull his arms from my legs and squat down next to Holland. Evan looks at me through tear-filled eyes. His death grip on Pickles hasn't lessened but at least he's looking at me.

"Buddy, can I tell you a secret? One that I haven't ever told anyone? My biggest secret?"

Evan looks from me to Holland then nods.

"When I was little, I had bad dreams. Just like you do. I was so afraid of the dark, I'd lie awake staring at the ceiling all night. But you know what? My mom once told me that being brave comes from in here." I press against his heart and he looks down at my finger. "Yep. Your brave in here, Evan. No matter what you face, no matter how scary it is. All you have to do is remember how brave you are in your heart."

Holland's eyes soften and she continues to rub Evan's back as he calms.

"I can be brave," Evan mumbles.

"You *are* brave, buddy. It's okay to be afraid sometimes because you have me, and together, we can be brave. We can face anything."

Even though we're standing in the middle of a boat dock, probably blocking everyone behind us, it doesn't matter. It all fades away because in this moment, Evan needed us.

He needed the reassurance that everything would be okay and that he was safe. And no matter where we go, or where we are, I will always stop to make sure he feels safe and protected.

Now that he's calmed down, the tears have dried, and he's seemingly okay, he surprises me when he leaps forward and throws his arms around my neck, squeezing tightly.

"I wuv you, Weed."

Jesus, someone's cutting onions again. My heart constricts in my chest with something I never thought I'd ever experience. I lift my arms and wrap them around his tiny body, and we stay like that. Embracing. Me fighting back misty eyes, and Holland gazing at us with tears in hers.

"I love you too, buddy."

We spend the rest of the day on the enormous replica of a ship, and thankfully, Evan has a great day. He laughs and plays, and the tears are a thing of the past. No more meltdowns. If anything, he seems lighter.

It's a good day.

The best day I've had in a long time, really.

Evan and Holland somehow talk me into wearing a pirate hat for a photo and all I can think about is how the guys are going to talk so much shit when they see it, but I don't even care. It made him happy, and that's all that matters. I'd wear an entire damn pirate costume if that's what it took to make him smile.

We're sitting at an Italian restaurant nestled right in the heart of Boston. It's quaint and cozy but still bursting with patrons. The place is boisterous, the wine is aged to perfection, and the food is mouthwatering. It's also only a few blocks over from our hotel, which makes getting back easier.

Our flight was set to leave tonight, but after the day we had, we both decided to reschedule it for tomorrow. Holland was able to talk to her dad's nurse and ask her to stay an additional day, and it isn't like I had anything pressing I had to rush home to. Evan was having a blast and I'd seen him smile more in the past day than I have since he's been with me. I wanted to hold on to that.

We're two glasses of wine in and Evan's passed out against Holland's side with her arm tucked around him, his mouth half-open, snoring lightly. He's exhausted. The little guy almost passed out in his plate of spaghetti. Neither one of us seem to want the night to end, so we've been talking over our finished plates for the past thirty minutes.

I don't know if it's the wine or the city lights, but Holland's eyes seem to shine each time she laughs, which she has been doing nonstop tonight.

Like right now, she's making fun of me after I told her a story about the lengths I go to, to make Liam's girls happy.

"Oh God, I'm seriously imagining you in a Frozen dress and a wig right now."

Probably shouldn't have told her that story because now I'll never live it down.

"Please don't. Look, I did it for the girls. You didn't see their faces, okay? I drew the line with lipstick."

Hollands laughs, low and sultry, and brings the wineglass to her lips. Who knew drinking wine could be so fucking sexy? There are lots of things that I didn't realize were a turn-on until Holland did them.

I'm way in over my damn head, and the smart thing would be to end it now. Put us all on a flight back home and find a sixty-year-old woman with gray hair and dentures to come on the road with Evan and me.

But, I'm selfish. So I won't.

I want every single second I can with Holland.

"Tell me about the future. For you. For Evan. What's your plan?" she says, taking another sip of wine. "You seem to already be figuring things out. I'm proud of you, Reed."

I drag my hand over my beard. "The truth?"

She nods.

"I don't know. One second my world was one way, then the next, Evan was thrust into it, and I don't have a plan. I just know that I'm thankful that things happened the way that they did. Not that my sister being murdered is what I wanted to happen, just that Evan came to live with me. Maybe at first I was hesitant and nervous, but now? I know this is exactly how things were supposed to happen. I'm going to continue to play hockey and spend all of my free time with Evan. Except for when Ma and Emery steal him for a sleepover. They're obsessed."

Holland smirks. "You know you stand no chance against Emery. She was made to be an aunt. She's been texting me images of things from Amazon all day today for his new room."

I gave Holland and Emery free rein, and they decided to make Evan's bedroom into a sea-themed room. I'm just handing over my AmEx and knowing my sister, I'll be a lot less rich when she's done.

"I just want to be there. Present. And be everything Ma raised me to be and nothing like my father." Thinking about him sends a swirl of unease to my gut. "That's what's important to me. I'm not going to have the answers to everything, and I'll probably have to call Ma, more often than not, but at least I'm here and I'm trying. I'm giving it everything I got."

My eyes drift to Evan, who's sleeping peacefully despite the bustle of the restaurant, and I smile. "Plus, he's a great little guy. I love him already. Makes it easy, ya know?"

"Definitely. He's infectious." She strokes his head affectionately.

The waiter walks up with the check. "Thank you for dining with us tonight. Enjoy your evening."

Once he's gone, I realize how late it's gotten. "I guess we should probably head back, get him in bed."

Holland nods and reaches for her wallet on the other side of her.

"You're crazy, let me treat you to dinner." I stop her by putting my card down on the check.

"Are you sure? I can pay for myself, Reed."

That's who she is. It's one of the things I've admired about her since we were younger.

"I know you can, but I'm offering, and I want to buy you dinner."

We get the check taken care of, and I put my coat on then take Evan from her. He immediately drops his head to my shoulder and falls back asleep before we're even outside the restaurant. Holland opens the door and we start our walk back to the hotel together. She stares at the tall buildings in awe as we pass by. "This place is incredible. It's mind-blowing to me that there's this entire world outside of Chicago that I haven't seen. It makes me want to add a dozen other things to my bucket list."

"It's one of the things I love about being able to travel for hockey. I get to see places that I love and places I've never seen. I'm glad you and Evan are here too. It's different with you here."

She's quiet for a moment then speaks, "Me too."

Once we get back to the hotel, Holland disappears into her

room for the night, and I get Evan ready for bed, putting him in his pajamas and brushing his teeth. After, he falls asleep quickly. Today wore him out, in the best way, and I'm hoping it means no nightmares.

I take a quick shower and change into a pair of old sweats, turning on ESPN before climbing into bed. A few minutes pass and then there's a soft knock on the adjoining door to Holland's room.

"Come in."

Holland opens the door and peeks her head around the corner. "Do you have a second?"

"Yeah, of course, are you okay?"

She's still behind the door with only her head peeking out.

"Uh, well, this is so embarrassing, but I was trying to take off my necklace and it's really tangled in my hair from the wind today. Could you help me? I'm so sorry."

"Yeah, it was really windy today. Let me see."

I get up from the bed and walk over to where she's hiding behind the door. Her eyes drift to my chest and lower to the grey sweats I'm wearing then she quickly drags them back up.

"Gotta open the door if you want me to help." I smirk.

She chews on the inside of her cheek nervously, but steps out from behind the door with only a towel wrapped tightly around her.

Fuck, I wasn't expecting that.

"I'm sorry, I was about to step into the shower, and I didn't want to try and put my shirt back on and chance getting tangled in it. This is super awkward. I can probably just figure this out myself without bothering you." She's rambling now, but I let her.

It's fucking cute. She's obviously flustered and I have a feeling it has less to do with the necklace and more to do with me.

"Holland. Breathe. It's fine," I say softly, "turn around."

She turns slowly, revealing her delicate neck and the naked skin of her back. Her hands are in her hair, lifting it up to expose the tangled chain. My eyes scan the expanse of skin that I want to make my way down with my tongue, then back up to the slope of her shoulder.

I gingerly lift the flimsy chain from her neck and unhook it. When my fingers brush against her skin lightly, she shivers. A response that has my cock twitching beneath my sweatpants.

Fuck, how does something so innocent feel like so much... more?

Leaning closer, I pull the tangled pieces of hair from the chain, until it's free, and then slide my hands around to remove it from her neck.

She looks back over her shoulder at me, her pupils dilated with the same feeling that I feel, and murmurs, "Thank you."

When she turns to face me, her cheeks are red and the flush seems to spread from her cheeks down her chest to where she's covered with the towel. I wonder how far down it actually goes.

"Reed," she breathes.

I know. I don't even have to ask about the warning tone in her words, because I know. But, I don't fucking care. We've been dancing around this, pushing it away like it wasn't here, but I can't ignore it any longer.

"I should go."

I nod. She should. Doesn't mean I want her to.

Her eyes hold mine, but she nods then disappears back through the door, shutting it firmly behind her.

My ass hits the bed and I drop my head into my hands. Shit, I'm gonna fuck this up. I know it. She's Emery's best friend.

She's also the girl I can't stop thinking about.

The decision is easy. I just pray like fuck she feels the same way.

CHAPTER NINE
REED

It's too late to change my mind. Too late to turn back now. Too late to cross back over into the untouched territory that we once were.

Not when all that's separating everything I've been desperate for sits on the other side of this door. Fuck, I've tried to hold back. Tried to be the good guy, the one who makes the right choices, but I can't.

Not anymore. Not after tonight solidifying everything I've been feeling.

My knuckles rap against the door, once, twice, three times, and then it swings open, revealing Holland on the other side. Her cheeks are flushed red, her mouth slightly parted, completely caught off guard.

"Reed? What are you doing he-"

I don't give either of us a chance to think. Stepping forward, I close the distance between us, my hands sliding up her jaw, into the nape of her hair and pulling her to me. Then my mouth is on hers. Her soft body collides with mine, and she whimpers beneath my touch.

I kiss her like I'm dying of thirst, and fuck, I want to *drown* in her.

It's the kiss to end all kisses. The kind that ruins everyone before her.

This is reckless and a recipe for fucking disaster, but I don't care. Maybe I will later, maybe we both will.

But right now, all I want is to lose myself in the girl that I can't stop thinking about.

When she opens her mouth to let me in, I slide my tongue in and groan when she fists my shirt like she's holding on for dear life. My hands slide down her back to her thighs and I pick her up, stepping farther inside the room. I kick the door shut behind me, and her legs tighten around my waist.

"Wait, wait, wait." She pants, ripping her mouth from mine. Her deep blue eyes search mine, but then she's kissing me again. Like she can't stop. It's needy, desperate, everything I've felt for the past few days. Out of my mind for her. "We shouldn't do this. No, we *can't* do this, Reed," she says again.

"Don't give a shit." I kiss along the path of her jaw, down her neck, sucking until she's whimpering beneath me.

"Reed."

I pull back and look at her. "Stop thinking, Holland. Listen, I couldn't sit on the other side of that goddamn door for another second, thinking about you, obsessing about having you. I'm losing my fucking mind. I can't be around you and not touch you any longer."

Her mind is at war with her body, and I can see the flames in her eyes. The same decision I've battled with, but in the end, my need for her won out. "Tell me you don't want this. Tell me right now that you don't feel the same thing that I do. Say it and I'll walk away, walk out of this room and we can pretend it never happened."

She softens beneath me, pulling her lip into her mouth before speaking, "Emery will kill us. This... this will screw everything up. You know it will."

Maybe so, but it's a risk I'm willing to take. I want her, and I want her over and over until neither one of us feels deprived. Of course I don't want to hurt Emery or jeopardize her and Holland's friendship, but at the end of the day, what happens between the two of us has nothing to do with Emery.

"Please do not mention my sister when my dick is hard." I groan.

Holland laughs, but the movement presses her core right against the head of my cock that's straining in my shorts.

I hiss, dropping my forehead to her shoulder.

"Look, Holl, the ball is in your court. I think I've made it apparent that I want this, but you control the show. If you're uncomfortable and want to keep things the way they are, I respect that. I respect you and I understand."

Our gazes lock and her eyes are the color of the sky before

a storm, cloudy and dark. Either decision, either route we take... something changes.

"If we... If this happens, no one can know. Especially not Emery. This is important to me, and it's the only way I'll ... agree to this," Holland says.

"Fine. Sworn to secrecy. Scout's Honor." I hold up two fingers as I make the promise, and she rolls her eyes.

"I'm serious, Reed. There has to be... rules. If you really want to do this, there has to be rules. Rules keep everything straight. No blurred lines, no miscommunications. Simple. Easy. No complications, so no one gets hurt."

I sigh and set her down on the bed gingerly, taking a seat next to her. The last thing I want to do is stop, but maybe drawing a clear line will help the fact that we're both entering uncharted territory. Plus, I can't think straight when she's that close to my dick.

"Okay, fine. Rules. Hit me."

"Rule one: Don't fall in love."

I scoff. "Babe, I don't do relationships. I don't do feelings. So, I don't think that'll be a problem for me."

Holland tears her gaze from mine, fiddling with her hands in her lap. "Feelings complicate things, and the last thing you need is a complication, and the last thing I want is to ruin the relationship I have with my one and only best friend. So, we both agree? Sex only."

"Done."

"Rule two: No one can ever know. I mean it, Reed. Not your

teammates, not Liam, and especially not Emery."

I nod. "I know. I'm a private guy, Holland, you have nothing to worry about."

And she doesn't. It's not like I'd stand on a rooftop and tell the world who I'm sleeping with. Briggs might, but not me. I respect Holland too much to ever purposefully put that shit on display.

"Do you have anything you want to add?"

Fuck, all I can think about it is getting my hands on her, but since we are having this conversation, I want to make my expectations clear. I hate miscommunication and the last thing I would ever want to do is hurt her.

"Rule three... When the season is over, we walk away. We go back to the way things were before."

Holland's face changes slightly and I think I almost see a flash of hurt, but she nods. "I agree. It's obvious we have some kind of chemistry, but it would never work outside of this. You're right. And I just... I don't want to lose Em, Reed."

"So, we stick to the rules. Strictly sex between friends."

"Okay. So..." she trails off, looking more nervous now that "the talk" is out of the way.

"There's no pressure, Holland, we take things at our own pace. Whatever you're comfortable with. No expectations."

The rules seem simple laid out this way, but I have a feeling they're going to be anything but simple.

Not when Holland is involved.

"How about we just watch a movie? I'm sure you have gummy

worms stashed somewhere in that suitcase since you're an addict. We can put something on and just... I don't know, hang out?" I ask.

Her deep blue eyes roll. "You don't know that."

I raise my eyebrows. "Are there gummy worms in your suitcase right now, Holland?"

"Fine."

She climbs off the bed, disappearing back into her suite, then returns with a giant bag of sour gummy worms. The same snack she's been addicted to since we were kids. She and Emery used to beg me to pick some up when I went grocery shopping for Ma, when they were having a sleepover.

Hesitantly, she crawls back onto the bed, taking her place next to me. I turn off the bedside lamp and put on a movie from pay-per-view. Something horror, since I know that she loves anything scary.

"Oh, I've been wanting to see this. It's the sequel to the first doll movie," Holland murmurs.

The movie starts and about halfway into it, Holland inches slightly closer. Then a little closer whenever a part makes her jump, until she's pressed against me. I'm trying to focus on the movie and not the feel of her, but she's making it hard.

And when I say it, I mean my dick.

That was a bad joke, but in all seriousness, I can't remember the last time I wanted anyone the way that I want Holland.

"I can't concentrate," she says.

"Me either."

She sits up on her elbows and plops another gummy worm in her mouth. "It's not like either of us is actually going to watch any of this movie. Let's play twenty questions. You ask a question, then I'll ask a question. We can get to know each other better."

"You've known me since you were seven, I'm pretty sure you know everything about me."

"Not true." She sits up completely and crosses her legs in front of her, and I have to force my eyes to stay on hers. "I'll go first. Favorite food?"

Shit, starting with the hard stuff right off the top.

I scratch my beard. "Probably Captain Crunch."

"You know, for a professional athlete with more muscles than anyone I've ever met, you eat a lot of sugar. I bet that drives Liam nuts."

My best friend hates sugar with every fiber of his being. So much so that he doesn't allow it in the house, except now that he has Juliet, she's changed the rules a little.

"Yeah, well, I'm a big guy, I need sustenance and not from fucking kale. That shit is gross."

She nods in agreement. "You're right. It tastes like a musty sock."

That makes me chuckle and then I decide to push her limits. Pull her out of her comfort zone. "What turns you on?"

My question catches her off guard, and she fidgets with the bag of candy in her hands. "Uh, I don't know."

"Yes, you do. C'mon, Holl. You want this between us? I want to know what you like, what turns you on." I lean closer until I can feel her hot breath against my lips, and then grin when she sucks in a sharp breath. "I want to know how I can make you light up, how I can make you come with my name on your lips."

She whispers hoarsely, "Kiss me."

My lips are on hers in the next breath, and together, we're fumbling to get her into my lap. I feel like I'll starve if I wait another second. *Fucking covers.* Finally, she's seated on me without ever breaking free from our kiss. Her hips jerk as she writhes against me, and I'm two seconds from losing it.

Her skin is hot and silky beneath my touch as my hands slide up her hips to her rib cage. Things are getting heated, fast. She's rocking against me, panting against my lips. Our movements are desperate, unhinged. Both of us coming together in a frenzy.

I'm going to fucking regret this, I know I am. But I'm a good guy and I respect her.

I tear my lips from hers and say her name roughly, "Holland, wait."

She immediately pulls back like cold water has been thrown on her, freezing in my lap.

My hands slide up her jaw to keep her looking at me. "Don't get lost in your head. I just want you to be sure that this is what you want. I don't want you to feel pressured."

"I don't feel pressured, but you're right. Maybe we should take baby steps. I just... I want this."

I nod. "I do too, babe. Let's just do like you said, baby steps.

Slow and steady."

I say the words, knowing I've never done anything small in my life, but I'm willing to try for Holland.

"How about we try this…" I lay her down on the bed before me and drop a light kiss against her collarbone. Then one to the swell of her breast peeking out from her tank top. Each time my lips connect with her skin, she gasps, a soft airy sound that makes me want to shove my fucking foot in my mouth for stopping earlier.

My fingers slide up her calves, to the inside of her thighs, drawing small circles on the tender flesh. Her muscles are taut. I can feel the hesitation in her body, and I want to make it disappear.

I look up at her from my position and ask, "Is this okay?"

She nods her head fervently, and I continue to trail my fingers upward until they brush against her pussy. The lightest of movements and her body responds eagerly, and if I didn't know it before, I know now… being with Holland is going to be a game changer. She's so responsive, and so pliant from my touch, it drives me insane.

This time, my fingers brush against her pussy, causing her to hiss.

"Is this okay?" I ask.

"Yes." Her voice is low and sultry, a raspy whisper.

I drag the sleep shorts down her hips, revealing a pair of lacy pink panties that almost make me want to fucking weep. Light pink and tiny, barely covering her slit. I don't ever think I've wanted something so badly. Not the way I want Holland.

Our eyes connect and her stormy blue irises seem hazy with lust, just the same as I'm feeling. Sliding my fingers under the thin strap of the lacy fabric, I hook them and pull them down past her hips and feet and toss them to the side.

Fuck, she's perfect.

My fingers explore her rosy, glistening pussy. Pink and pouty and perfect. I can't wait to put my mouth on her and taste her, but I want to go slow and give her time to get used to the fact that this will be happening... a lot. I plan to spend every free moment I have worshipping her. Because a woman like Holland deserves to be worshipped.

I use my fingers to part her, opening her up so I can admire every inch of her. Starting with the sensitive little nub of her clit. When I place my finger on it and rub gently, her hands come down to fist in my hair.

"Oh," She breathes. Simple, but the way the word tumbles from her lips, it's the most erotic thing I've ever heard. I lightly tease her clit with my finger and then trail it down, replacing my pointer with my thumb and then slowly sliding my finger inside her. She's so fucking tight, her pussy is clamped down on me and I bite back a curse.

So tight, and wet, I fuck her with my fingers. Slowly. Taking my time to savor this moment.

Hooking my finger up, I rub along the spot that makes her back bow from the bed, and her hands in my hair yank furiously.

"Reed, God, more," she pants, and I give her more.

I add a second finger, and rub her clit in sync.

"That's it, Holland, let go, I want to feel you come on my hand."

When the words leave my mouth, she squeezes her eyes shut and stops fighting. Her hands fist my hair roughly, and she rides my hand. Completely wild and unashamed. She comes so hard her entire body trembles with pleasure, her pussy clenches tightly around my fingers and her moan echoes around the edges of the room. I bring my free hand up to cover her mouth, and now the sounds vibrate against my hand.

I'm so goddamn hard I feel like I might bust through my sweats.

Once her body has gone slack and she's slowly letting go of my hair, I remove my hand from her mouth and her cheeks redden.

"Don't be embarrassed, baby, that was fucking amazing," I tell her. I pull my fingers from her pussy and bring them to my mouth, sucking the taste of her from them, and her eyes widen in shock.

"You taste amazing, and next time? I'm worshipping your pussy with my fingers and my mouth."

"Oh my God," she breathes, "did this really just happen?"

"It did, and if I have it my way, it's going to happen again. Over and over."

We crossed the line tonight, and now... we can never go back.

And I have no intention of ever trying to.

CHAPTER TEN
HOLLAND

In all of the years I've known Reed, I've never seen him play in an arena, until tonight.

The arena itself could probably fit our entire small town in it. To say it's massive would be an understatement. I feel tiny sitting in the seats that Reed got us. My eyes drift to him on the ice. Fans chant his name, the air around us is electrifying. You can *feel* the buzz of excitement and it's indescribable.

It's amazing. It's more thrilling than anything I've ever experienced.

"Weed on the ice?" Evan asks. He plops another organic gummy in his mouth and chews.

I laugh. "Yes, Evan, Reed is on the ice. See." I point toward Reed, who's in the center of the ice with the puck. His jersey hangs on his broad shoulders with his last name adorned on the back.

Jesus, the man is sex on a stick. Literally. I can't pull my eyes off of him as he races across the ice. There's no doubt that he was born to be a hockey player. From an early age, everyone around him knew that he was something special. It wasn't just a hobby for him; Reed has a gift. As kids, he spent the majority of his time on the ice or working out. I spent enough days hanging around with Emery to know how talented he was. We watched every night as he and his friends played games against each other until the sun went down.

Thankfully, over the years, I've picked up enough general hockey knowledge to keep up with the game. The entire time Evan watches excitedly, still clutching Pickles, of course, and he bounces in his seat when the crowd cheers and claps when a goal is made.

Anxiously, I watch Reed in his element, gliding across the ice with ease and a finesse that comes from ability, not just practice. He handles the puck masterfully, weaving between players until he's lined up for the shot.

I'm chewing my nails to the quick as the clock ticks down, second by second, and I switch from watching Reed to checking the time that's dwindling.

God, no one told me this could be so nerve-wracking. I'm on the edge of my chair.

One guy from the opposite team seems to get the puck from Reed one too many times, because even from here, I can see the determination that flashes on his face. He's done messing around.

Faking left, he swipes the puck and darts right before the big idiot can stop him, then he's racing down the ice toward the goal.

I hold my breath as he lines up for his shot, and he lets it fly.

The crowd erupts, and I expel the breath I was holding deep

in my lungs. Holy shit, Reed just scored the winning goal. His teammates surround him and slap him on the back, everyone's screaming. Evan is jumping up and down in his seat. It's pure chaos, but the kind that you want to be lost in.

It's a moment that even months from now, when whatever this is, is over, when we've both gone back to how our lives were before, I won't forget. Above us, the jumbotron zooms in on Reed's face. He's so devastatingly handsome, and even if he wasn't, the amount of charm he possesses would make any girl melt at his feet.

My heart flips in my chest as I watch everyone cheer for him and I wish, if only for a second, that I could celebrate with him. In public, with the world watching, not tucked away as a secret. I know that my hopes are silly, but my heart seems to believe in false hope and silly dreams.

I tamper down the feeling, and look over at Evan, who's still grinning ear to ear and clutching Pickles. I'm glad that he's finally starting to come out of his shell some. We both watch Reed and the team on the jumbotron, a permanent giddy grin plastered on my lips, and then Reed does something I don't expect.

He turns toward the crowd, where he knows we're seated, and he winks. I can see it in HD, the sly grin that shows his dimples and the wink that has the butterflies in my stomach fluttering wildly. He holds his hand up in a wave, and while the crowd erupts, thinking it's for them, I know it's for us.

Evan and I make our way down the stands and to the back where we're supposed to meet Reed. There is media everywhere with microphones and cameras, waiting to catch a glimpse of the guys as they leave the locker room, so we wait to the side. We play a game of hide and seek, using a row of benches, and Evan's delighted giggle rings out through the swarm of reporters. A few minutes later, after their post-game meeting, Reed comes strolling through the door with his bag slung over his shoulder, wearing a black tee and faded jeans.

"Did you see that shot?" he says when he makes it over to us. Bending down, he gives Evan a high five and a fist bump, then stands to his full height to face me.

I grin. "Of course I saw it. You were incredible, Reed."

"Fuck, I feel on top of the damn world right now." He fist-pumps the air. "It hasn't felt that good on the ice in a long time. I needed this. Let's get out of here."

He bends down and picks up Evan, so he can carry him through the crowd, and once we're surrounded by the sea of people trying to leave the stadium, he holds out his hand behind him. I hesitantly slide mine into it. From an outsider's perspective, it may look a tad suspicious, but it's easily defended as he's simply helping me through the crowd.

It doesn't stop the sinking, awful feeling in my stomach from replacing the butterflies he'd just given me. I haven't been able to stop thinking about it since we came up with the rules for this agreement. The fact that there is even an agreement or the fact that Reed wants me as more than just his little sister's best friend, is *a lot* to process.

And Emery has been in the back of my mind the entire time. I can't imagine what her reaction would be if she found out that I'm selfishly breaking the promise I made her so long ago to put our friendship first and to never think about Reed this way.

I hate to think of myself as selfish, but at the same time, there's never been a time when I put myself or what I've wanted first. Until now.

Until Reed.

For the first time in my life, I'm putting me first. That's why it's important to me to keep this casual, to put an expiration date on things, and to make sure things remain uncomplicated. That way, Emery will never know. Things won't change. It's just sex. Then we walk away.

"Holl?"

When I look up, Reed is staring at me with his brow furrowed. Evan is lying on his shoulder, completely passed out.

Oh god, the two of them together is too much to take. It's adorable.

This is what women mean when they say baby fever. It's never been a thing until I see Reed Davidson clutching a sleeping toddler to his chest.

"Sorry, the crowd was crazy, I kind of zoned-out. I can't believe he fell asleep through that."

Reed grins. "Call me the baby whisperer."

I roll my eyes and laugh. It's freezing outside, in the low forties, so Reed transfers a sleepy Evan into my arms, and leaves us in the warmth while he waits for the Uber. It finally pulls up to the curb, and I realize how exhausted I am. The adrenaline from the game has left me feeling drained, and I can't wait to crawl into the plush sheets of the hotel's bed.

"Ready?" Reed appears back through the doors.

I nod. I don't want to wake Evan, so I keep quiet until we're inside the car and buckled. The ride back to the hotel is quiet, even though I see Reed's knee bouncing nonstop. He's completely amped up, still riding the high from his win.

We arrive at the hotel a few minutes later, and thankfully, this time the elevator is working because I did not feel like climbing three flights of stairs with the dead weight of a sleeping toddler in my arms.

My room is next to Reed's, so once the elevator dings and we're on our floor, I follow Reed inside their suite and put Evan in bed, making sure to take off his shoes and tuck Pickles back into his arms.

I hear the shower running as I close the door to his room and walk back into Reed's.

I'm unsure what to do. Do I stay? Would Reed want that? Everything between us is so new, I don't know what to do in a situation like this. I nervously chew on the inside of my lip, a habit I'm desperately trying to break, when Reed walks out of the bathroom with a white towel wrapped around his waist. He's dry, so he must have not showered yet.

Jesus Christ.

My eyes drift from his dimpled, playful grin down the hard planes of his chest to the set of abs that are enough to make my mouth water. I'm a goner when it comes to this man, and he knows it, judging by the smug expression on his face.

"Just gonna stand there, babe? Or..." He trials off, waiting for my answer. Reed is so effortlessly confident and I'm... not.

Suddenly, I feel shy, the old Holland resurfacing at the worst possible time. What happened to the brazen and bold Holland who took charge the other night? The one who wasn't afraid or self-conscious as Reed devoured my body.

"I- I wasn't sure you wanted me to stay," I whisper.

Reed's expression morphs into confusion, then he laughs. "You don't need an invitation, Holland. We've made it clear where we stand with each other, and babe, I want you. I want you now, tomorrow, a fucking week from now."

My cheeks burn with his admission, but my clit throbs, needy and desperate for his attention.

He stalks forward and pulls me toward him, capturing my lips in a kiss that causes me to melt against him. His lips are firm and plush, and when his tongue slips inside my mouth, all of my doubt and hesitation, all of my worries disappear to where the only thing I can feel is Reed. I feel how hard he is pressed against me, and my hands travel down his chest to the knotted towel at his waist. I brush my hand against his cock, and he hisses loudly in response.

"Fuck, Holland."

Gathering every single ounce of confidence inside me, I drop to my knees before him and look up under my lashes.

"Holland, I don't expect this," Reed starts, but I shake my head, stopping him.

"I want this. I've wanted to do this for so long."

His gaze turns molten, burning straight through me. When his long, thick fingers wrap around my throat gently, moving up to my jaw, he swipes the rough pad of his thumb across my bottom lip. His touch is encouraging and reassuring. It gives me the push to continue.

I undo the towel at his waist, and it falls to the floor in a pile. His cock springs free, bobbing in my face, and I eagerly wrap my shaking hand around him. He's so thick and girthy, my fingers don't meet as I grip him.

The best thing about having Reed as a lover? He's vocal. I've learned that from only our first time together, and it's something I never realized I wanted so badly.

Pumping my fist, I work his cock up and down, and use my tongue to trace his sensitive head. He immediately weaves his hand in my hair, letting out a low, tortured groan. I look up at him and see his head thrown back as he grips my hair, and only then do I close my mouth around him and suck until my cheeks hollow.

Every time I suck him deeper into my mouth, he tightens his grip in my hair. After a few moments, he pulls back abruptly, panting.

"Goddamn, Holland, I am not going to last, stop." He pleads, breathlessly.

God, he's so handsome.

He extends his hand toward me. "Come shower with me. Please?"

I nod and place my hand in his. When I get to my feet, he slides his hands under my sweater, against my stomach, and trails them up, until he's pulling the fabric over my head and tossing it aside. He kisses me as he unclasps my bra, letting my breasts spill free.

It's always the thing I'm most conscious about, my stomach and breasts. I'm not rail thin; I have hips, thighs, and an ass. My breasts are heavy and full. I always shy away from this moment, but Reed's gaze on my body makes me feel anything but self-conscious.

"You are perfect. I can't get enough. These," he cups my breasts in his hands, and they almost cover them fully. A perfect handful for Reed, "they're made for me, for my hands, for my lips. Mine."

He bends down and pulls my nipple into his mouth and rolls it between his tongue and teeth. The sensation is enough to cause my knees to go weak. He scrapes his teeth lightly against the sensitive tip and I shudder.

"Reed," I pant. Pulling back, he looks at me. His deep chocolate eyes are locked on mine, and his breathing is labored just as mine is. Something passes between us, something I can't place, but now I feel closer to him than ever.

He quickly removes my jeans, and the sheer satin panties I have on, leaving me completely bare in front of him. Out of habit, I want to cover myself, and when I move to, he catches my hand.

"Don't. Don't hide yourself from me. I want you, Holland,

every single fucking inch of you."

The words cause me to shiver in a lusty haze. He reaches down and picks me up then carries me into the bathroom, directly to the shower. The hot water has been going, so the walls are steamed over, and it billows from the scalding water.

Reed steps inside, lowering me to my feet once we're under the spray. It feels heavenly, almost as good as the feel of his hands on me, but I haven't felt anything that compares to the way Reed touches me.

That thought scares me. It terrifies me that when I'm with Reed… I feel so much. How powerless I become, falling for his charm.

He takes my chin in his fingers and tips my head up to look at him. "Get out of your head. Don't let anything in the space between us right now. Feel us."

I nod. He picks up the shampoo he put in the shower and squirts a generous amount into his hands and then puts it in my hair. Without warning, my body melts into his touch. He massages the shampoo into my scalp, washing it completely.

It's intimate in a way that I've never experienced. Washing my hair, treating me tenderly with such care. After he's done, he drops to his knees before me, just as I was only minutes ago.

I look at him questioningly, and he nuzzles his nose against my hip before kissing the spot where it dips. A spot I've hated for as long as I can remember, but suddenly, I've never loved it more. He dips his tongue inside my belly button.

Nothing has ever felt so erotic. Standing under a scalding spray, Reed still makes me shiver. With need. I'm caught in a fever dream and I never want to wake up. He continues his path lower until he reaches my pussy. Then, he lifts my leg to his shoulder, causing me to grip onto his hair to remain upright.

"Reed," I cry.

"Shh, babe, I've got you."

And then he uses his fingers to part my folds and lowers his mouth to my clit. The second his tongue flicks the sensitive, throbbing nub, I buck against his mouth.

Oh. My. God.

Reed Davidson is devouring me on his knees in the shower. I've had dreams of this very moment. For years, I've imagined this exact scenario in my head and now I know that nothing, and I mean nothing, compares to the real thing.

As one hand grips my hip and the other parts my pussy lips, he eats me like he's been starving all day to do so. He laps at my pussy, sucking my clit into his mouth, and I can't stop the moan that escapes my mouth. Pleasure like I've never known blossoms inside me, spilling into my limbs, making it even harder to stay upright.

Reed senses it because he stops abruptly, turning the water off and opening the shower door. Again, he scoops me off my feet. I'm soaking wet and dripping all over the floor, but it doesn't faze him; he carries me into the room and tosses me on the bed. I don't even have time to speak before he's pulling me to the edge of the bed, so he can kneel on the floor.

He takes a long, languid swipe with his tongue from my entrance to my clit and my hands fist in the sheets, an anchor for the pleasure he's pulling from my body.

Effortlessly.

My eyes roll back in my head as he dips his tongue inside me, thrusting in and out as he adds his thick finger, curving up and rubbing against the spot that has my back arching off the bed. His beard rubs against my thighs as he devours me, and I know for sure that I'll feel him there tomorrow, a delicious burn that will be a steady reminder of this moment of pleasure.

"You are so responsive, fuck, it's amazing," he says between my thighs as he pushes another finger inside me.

I feel the waves of my orgasm cresting and when he sucks my clit into his mouth, hard, I crash.

My back bows and my hands abandon the sheets and fist into his hair instead, pulling him closer against me as the most powerful orgasm I've ever felt consumes my body. He continues to languidly fuck me with his fingers, alternating with his tongue, until my body is spent, and I'm a pile of bones.

I sink into the bed, sated and blissful in my post-orgasmic state.

Reed crawls up my body, my wetness still coating his beard and lips, and it's so dirty… so erotic, that even after the best orgasm I've ever had, I want more. I want him, over and over, until we can't any longer.

"Are you exhausted?"

He lies down beside me, gathering me in his arms. "Now? Yeah."

I giggle.

"After a game, especially one like tonight, I'm usually wired. It's the adrenaline, it takes a long time to wear off. I used to go out with the guys, or find other ways to work off the energy. But... I prefer to work it off this way."

"I thought I was tired before we got back, now, I'm exhausted. I need to get dressed and get back to my room. I need to repack before we leave tomorrow."

"Stay? Just for a bit. We can rest our eyes."

I sigh sleepily. One minute won't hurt. Then, tomorrow, we'll be home. And we will go back to pretending that there's nothing between us.

Easier said than done.

CHAPTER ELEVEN
HOLLAND

Reed: Did you know that octopuses have three hearts?

read the message again to make sure I've read it right. Why is Reed texting me about octopuses at midnight? Setting my paperback aside, I respond.

Me: I did not, but I guess I do now. LOL.

A few seconds later, the gray hovering dots appear, showing he's responding.

Reed: They also have nine brains. One in each tentacle. (Octopus emoji)

Me: Wow. Pickles must be a smart guy then.

Reed: No kidding. What are you up to?

It's strange texting Reed. We've lived next door to each other and grown up together our entire lives, but we've never had a casual relationship where we text or talk outside of my time at his house with Emery.

We've been home from Boston for two days now. Two extremely long days that I haven't seen or really spoken to him.

But, since the rules are clearly defined for "us," I didn't want to seem clingy. I plan to see him the day after tomorrow when we leave for his game in Vancouver.

I've spent the past two days with my dad. And now, I feel even guiltier, knowing the last few have been rough ones. He spent the majority of the day calling me, Annie, my mother. I hated that I was spending time away from him.

Me: Just lying in bed reading, nothing exciting. What about you?

A few seconds later, my phone rings, and it's Reed on FaceTime. I dart up in bed, panicking. My hair is in a messy, two-day old bun on the top of my head. I have zit cream on, and a nightgown that has Care Bears on it from an embarrassingly long time ago.

Oh my god. I fumble with my phone, dropping it onto the rug next to my bed, but quickly retrieve it and decline the call.

He cannot see me like this. No way. I'll die of embarrassment.

Before I can even type a text to him, my phone dings.

Reed: You going to pretend you don't have your phone in your hand right now? Or are you going to answer?

Busted.

Shit. Shit. Shit. SHIT.

I scramble from the bed and sprint to the bathroom. I quickly run a brush through my hair, and wash off all remnants of zit cream before grabbing an old hoodie from high school and throwing it on.

I still look homeless, but it's considerably better than five minutes ago. My phone rings again, and I lie down on the bed before answering.

Reed's face comes into view and he smiles; his dimples pop, causing those stupid butterflies to break loose again.

"Finally."

I laugh nervously. "I, uh, had to get decent."

God, that sounded stupid. *Get your shit together, Holland*.

He laughs. "Decent, huh? You read in the nude? Now that is a sight I'd pay to see. Can you read to me naked? I'm thinking maybe Harry Potter while I eat your pu-"

My eyes widen, and I immediately screech, "Oh my god, Reed!"

I reach over to my nightstand and put in my AirPods because hearing Reed say that out loud causes my cheeks to flame. My body suddenly feels on fire.

"Sorry, babe, that's going in the spank bank for life."

I hide my face with a blanket while he laughs. This conversation just took a turn that I was not expecting. I don't want him to see my cheeks bright red from blushing.

Changing the subject, I say, "So, um, have you been studying octopuses?"

Reed leans back against the headboard and shakes his head. "Nah, Evan saw the octopus on *Finding Nemo* and made me rewind it ten times, so I pulled up YouTube and we watched and learned random facts about octopuses. Kept him quiet for like an hour."

I love hearing about Reed's relationship with Evan. I have more respect and admiration for him now than ever before. Not many men would do what Reed did, especially not at the peak of their career and with the world at their fingertips. He's a good man. The best man, and I've always known that. It's just different seeing him interact with Evan.

The thoughts in my head feel too intimate. Too much for this conversation, so I clear my throat. "What's up with the late-night call? Is there something we need to discuss for tomorrow?"

He runs his big, surly hand through his mop of dark hair before shaking his head. "Maybe I missed you, babe."

God, the butterflies in my stomach are fluttering wildly right now. Why does he have to be *this* charming? He makes it so easy to feel things that I shouldn't, that I *can't.*

"Did you?"

He shrugs. "Yeah, I did. Probably against the rules, but I've always been a rule breaker."

I laugh. It feels good. The ease I feel with Reed. But, it's also easy to forget that there are rules in place for a reason, and as much as I wish things were different, they won't be, can't be. I have to protect my heart too.

"Maybe I missed you too."

His lips tug up in a playful smirk. "Just maybe? Damn."

Unable to stop it, I yawn. "God, I'm exhausted. I have a huge test to study for so I need to get some sleep. Em's going to help me study tomorrow night. But I'll see you on Friday? Okay?"

"Good luck on your test. Night, babe."

My heart skips slightly at his favorite name for me lately. "Night, Reed."

I press the end button, exiting FaceTime, but even after he's gone... I find myself still thinking of Reed, and maybe... definitely missing him too.

Rules be damned.

I spend the majority of the next day running errands, grocery shopping, and taking care of things around the house to make sure that when I head on the road again that my dad has everything he needs. This morning I had a talk with his nurses, and they assured me everything's okay, and they have it under control, but I still worry. It's who I am. I've spent the better part of my teenage and adult life worrying about him.

Guilt still sits heavy in the pit of my stomach.

Bringing the coffee to my lips, I take another sip, praying that it starts to work because my brain feels like it may be on the verge of crashing sometime soon.

I sigh and drop my head onto the textbook in front of me. Just when I think I've got it down, I begin to second-guess myself and the vicious cycle continues.

"You need a break. You're doing yourself no good like this," Emery says as she sits across from me. We've been at it for hours, and I feel no more prepared than I did when I sat down.

Maybe she's right, maybe I'm putting too much pressure on

myself.

"I feel like if I stare at this for even one more second, my head is going to explode."

"How about we go get a drink? Just step away for a second and then we'll come back and do another round."

"Okay, one hour. Then we come back. I have to ace this, Em."

Emery nods and thrusts my jacket at me. "Come on, it'll be super quick and give your brain a chance to relax."

We walk to Johnny's, a nearby sports bar that has food and drinks, and snag a booth near the front door. It's quiet for a Wednesday.

After taking her coat off, Emery orders us both a drink and an appetizer and then turns to face me. "So, how was the first time on the road with Reed and Evan? Tell me everything."

My heart speeds up in my chest. This is the part that I have been dreading like the plague. Shit, I don't want to lie to her and discussing Reed is withholding the truth. I don't think in all of the years that we've been friends, I've ever kept the truth from her.

I hate lying. And until now, I've never had anything to hide from Emery.

"Uh," I stammer, "it was great. Nothing special to report. You know Reed." I laugh nervously. God, this is not going to be easy. I swallow thickly, trying to push the guilt back down where it came from.

Thankfully, the waitress brings over our drinks and chips and salsa, saving me.

"How's work been going?"

Emery works for a law firm downtown, where she's going to be doing her internship after she graduates.

Her eyes, that are the same deep chocolate color as Reed's, light up at the mention of work. "Oh my god! I totally forgot to tell you. So, there's this paralegal that works on the third floor. He's super cute. Like tall, nerdy, but in a good way. He has amazing eyes and his smile is so perfect. Well, we got talking the other day and he asked if I wanted to go out. Duh, I totally said yes." She grins, raising her eyebrows. "And, he has a friend. We're totally setting you two up on a blind date."

My stomach drops, all the way out the bottom of the chair onto the floor. Not that Reed and I are anything beyond the friend with benefits thing, but I can't imagine seeing another guy while I'm sleeping with Reed. Not that it's part of the rules...

Which, also makes me feel like I might throw up because, until now, I didn't even think it would be something I needed to talk with Reed about. What if he's sleeping with other girls too?

Emery snaps her fingers in my face. "Hello? Holland?"

"Sorry, what?" I stutter, still obsessing over the scenario in my head.

"I said, when you get back next week, we're going to meet up and go on a double date. His friend is so dreamy. I think you two would get along so well. He's super into his job. He works at a children's hospital, I think. Anyway, what do you think?"

I think that I have to text Reed right now, or I'm just going to keep thinking about this. I have to make it clear that I'm not comfortable with him sleeping with anyone else.

"Sure, Em, sounds good," I say absentmindedly. It seems to appease her because she drops it and chows down on the chips and salsa.

I pull my phone from my bag and open my text exchange with Reed.

Me: This is random, sorry, but uh... this wasn't really discussed in our rules and I needed to know. Are you going to be sleeping with other girls, you know, while our arrangement is happening?

Waiting a few seconds to see if he opens it, I don't see the read status change, so I lock my phone and shove it back inside my purse. I'm overreacting. This is silly.

"You are on another planet tonight, babe," Emery says, shoving another chip in her mouth.

"I know, I'm sorry. I just have a lot going on."

There, not a lie, just... not the entire truth.

We finish our margaritas and chips, and then head back to my house. Emery's quieter on the way home, and I worry that I've upset her.

"You okay?" I bump her shoulder as we walk.

"Yeah, just didn't sleep great last night, I guess I was just excited. I'm going to spend the entire day with Evan tomorrow before you guys leave, and I can't wait! We had so much fun the last time, and I just love being able to spend time with him."

I nod. "He's a great little guy. Reed is lucky he has him."

After a short walk, we're back at my front door. Emery looks at me. "Get some studying done, but don't stress yourself out, okay? I'm going to head out and try to get some sleep."

"Okay. Love you, Em." I pull her in for a hug. She squeezes me back tightly before whispering, "I love you, too, Holl."

I didn't expect it to be so hard. Keeping the truth from my best friend.

CHAPTER TWELVE
REED

I never responded to Holland's text message. The one that came at almost midnight. Not because I had anything to hide, but because I didn't want to discuss something like me sleeping with someone else in a text message.

Am I interested in any other female that doesn't have long, honey blonde hair and sea-green eyes that keep me up at night? Fuck no.

And that worries me, but it doesn't change the fact that it's true.

We just checked into our hotel in Vancouver, and right now, I've got bigger problems.

Potty training problems. I shudder at the thought. Sure, I've changed enough diapers in my lifetime with Ari and Ken, Liam's daughters, to be able to do it in the dark, drunk, with my eyes closed.

But teaching a boy to pee in the toilet... and aim? Whole different hockey puck.

"Okay, so we're going to count to three and then you just, I don't know, aim for the water?"

Evan looks at me like I've grown two heads. He's standing on a stool in front of the toilet with his pants around his ankles, and honestly, he looks as worried as I feel.

I've spent the last thirty minutes googling tips for potty training, and I've come across some strange shit. And I'm just saying, my search history sure as shit looks a lot different than it used to. Potty.com is nothing like pornhub.com.

"Pee now?" Evan asks.

"Yeah, buddy, just try and make it into the bowl."

"Bowl? Cereal?"

I groan.

This is a disaster, and I don't know if I can solve it on my own. I look down at my phone again and before I can talk myself out of it, I dial the number.

"Hello?" Holland's breathless voice comes through the phone.

"Hey, uh," I stammer, "Can you come help me with something really quick?"

"Of course, yeah. Be there in a sec." The line goes dead and I exhale. Fuck yes, I want to see Holland, but I'm also not trying to make her feel overwhelmed or have to call her for every single little thing. I'm Evan's guardian. I have to figure shit out on my own.

Except this, because I'm obviously getting fucking nowhere. I mean, I have the same parts as him, and I still can't explain it to him.

Seconds later, there's a knock at the door.

"Don't move, okay, buddy?" I say.

Evan nods, hands on his hips, pants around his ankles.

If I wasn't so distraught over failing at this whole potty-training thing, I'd laugh.

I pad through the room and open the door for Holland. She smiles, but it quickly falls when she sees the look on my face.

"What's wrong? Is Evan okay?" Her words come out in a rush. She goes from happy to panicked so quickly that I pull her by her hand into the room.

"No, he's fine, I'm having a crisis."

I lead her into the bathroom to Evan, who's still waiting patiently on the stool.

Her eyes dart from me to him, then back. "Uh? Okay? So... we're pottying?" She laughs.

"Well, that's the plan, but he won't. He just keeps looking at me like I've lost my mind."

Holland is quiet for a few seconds, and then she tosses her head back and laughs. So loud that it echoes off the wall in the bathroom and causes Evan to laugh with her.

"Holland, c'mon, I'm serious. I've been searching online for an hour and it's telling me to get these books and treats and I just... fuck, I don't know. I feel like I'm failing at this." I exhale a frustrated breath.

She steps closer to me and slides her hands up my chest into my hair at the back of my neck. "First of all, take a breath. It's okay. Every parent goes through this, and you are not failing. You just have to figure it out, together."

"Alright. You're right."

"So, what most people do is Cheerios. Just toss 'em in there, and tell him to shoot for them. He'll figure it out."

Okay, Cheerios. Got it.

"Okay, I'll call down to concierge and see if they can send some up. Maybe we should pick this back up tomorrow." I nod at Evan, who's swaying slightly on the stool. His eyes beginning to droop.

Holland laughs, and then helps him down and gets his pull-up back on correctly. She helps him into his pajamas and he sighs sleepily when she picks him up, then lies his head on her shoulder.

"You're good at this, you know?"

She smiles. "He makes it easy. Let me put him down, and I'll be back."

I follow behind them back into the room, then sit on the bed and fall back.

Shit, parenting is hard. Rewarding as fuck, but still hard.

I've been thinking about my decision a lot lately, about taking Evan in, about my sister, about my father. I've got shit in my head I'm trying to work through because I want to be the best I can be for Evan.

I keep thinking about the fact that even though my father might not deserve it, what if I never get the chance to make things right with him? What if I spend all this time hating him, and then it's just over? And there's no closure. I still harbor all of this hurt from him abandoning our family to start a new one. But it doesn't hurt him; it hurts *me*. It changes *me*.

"Reed?"

My eyes fly open, and I see Holland standing over me, looking concerned. I sit up and pull her toward me. She falls easily into my arms.

"Are you tired?" she asks.

I shake my head. "Just thinking. About your text message."

She stills in my arms. After a second, she pulls back and looks at me with wide eyes. "I'm sorry that I texted that. I should've waited until I saw you."

"Don't apologize. Holland, I'm not an asshole. I know the rules, and if you want to add a fourth, we can, but right now, I'm not interested in anyone but you. Period."

"I'm not interested in anyone either. I just wanted to be clear that I'm not comfortable sleeping together if there are other girls."

"There's not. While we're together, it's just us."

I watch as her expression changes from guarded to relieved, and I feel like a dick. A dick that selfishly wants her all to myself, but not at the expense of damaging my relationship with my sister.

And truthfully, it isn't just Emery that causes me to pause. It's the fact that I'm not, and never have been, a relationship kind of guy. I've never had a serious relationship in my life, and I know that if I take things further with Holland, I'll just end up hurting her. Maybe I feel this way because of my father abandoning Ma. Maybe it runs in the family, I don't know. But I do know that I can't and won't hurt Holland, so this, whatever this is between us, is what it'll have to be.

"You wanna stay tonight?" I ask.

"I'm honestly exhausted. I've been studying for my exam so late every night. Tomorrow?"

"Yeah, babe, go get some sleep."

I lean down and kiss her for the first time tonight, and fuck, it hits me square in the chest. Nothing feels the way it does when I'm with her.

"Goodnight, Reed," she says before leaving me in my feelings, alone.

Fuck, I'm in way over my head.

We beat Vancouver three to one, and fuck, it feels good. There's nothing like performing your best and the entire damn world seeing it. And now I feel on top of the damn world.

Coach Rick is requiring me and Briggs to do some post-game interviews tonight, when all I want to do is get to Evan and Holland, but I know as soon as I get it done then I'm home free for the next two days.

I'm nursing my bottle of Gatorade as the reporters sit across from me. "So Reed, how are you feeling after that win?"

I plaster on my most charming smile before answering, "On top of the damn world."

Another round of cameras flash before a young girl in the back speaks. "Mr. Davidson, you've had one of the best years so far, stats wise, that you've ever had for the Avalanche. Anyone special you owe your success to?"

The question catches me off guard, but I quickly recover. "Maybe someone special." Followed by a wink.

Coach steps in. "That's enough for tonight. Thanks, everyone." He ushers Briggs and me from the chairs toward the side of the press room.

"Damn vultures, I swear. Good job tonight, Davidson, Wilson. Get some rest, I'll see you in a few days."

Briggs nods, and we walk over to where Asher, Graham, and Hudson are standing. Much like me, they're amped up from tonight's win.

"So, we heading out tonight? I need some bunny love," Graham says. He's eye-fucking a brunette from across the room, and I can tell he's out in full force tonight.

"When do you not?" Asher grins.

"Tell me about it," Briggs mutters.

Graham Adams is the rookie. The new kid, the fresh meat. Which means he's the one that we give all the shit to, and the one most likely to get a medal for fucking the most puck bunnies in a year. The kid has a thing with the ladies that half of us wish we had, but honestly, he's insane with a stick and a puck. I don't think I've ever seen someone skate as fast or as fluidly as he does. The only thing he doesn't have going for him? His mouth.

"Look, I can't help it if you're suffering from fucking your fist because you can't find a girl to fuck you, kinda problems. I'm good in that department."

"Adams, if you keep talking, I'm going to break your legs off and beat you with them."

I laugh. "I'm staying in tonight, gotta check on Evan." He and Holland remained at the hotel, since it was a later than normal game, and damn, I'm ready to be there with them.

"Don't you have a babysitter for that?" Hudson asks with his eyes glued to his phone. Asher elbows him for being a dick.

"First of all, she's not a babysitter, she's a family friend. Second, I don't expect her to keep Evan while I'm out partying."

Briggs nods. "Don't worry, I'll drink enough for the both of us."

The five of us walk side by side out of the arena and to the shuttle bus that will take us back to the hotel.

"Stay out of trouble. Why don't you come back to the hotel with me? We can grab a beer at the bar there. One that's not crawling with bunnies and reporters waiting for you to fuck up."

Briggs is still in deep shit with the team. He can't keep his ass out of fights or from making headlines. Mark, the owner, and our coach have had enough of the bad publicity. As his best friend, I'm just trying to keep his ass in line.

A dark look crosses his face. "I don't know why the media is up my ass all the time. I'm fucking over it."

"Because you've got too much talent to waste it," Asher says. He shoves his bag into the undercarriage of the bus. "You're the best forward I've ever seen, without a fucking doubt, but you're no good to the team if you're sitting out or, hell, off the damn team."

Briggs stays silent, his jaw clenched, before he brushes past us onto the bus without another word.

I know it's a grey area for him, fuck I get it, but Asher's right. If Briggs continues on this path, the only place he's going to be is home on his couch without a team.

"Nobody better call me tonight if you go to jail. Call Sam because I am unavailable." I grin.

"Can't help it, you're like the dad of the team. Suits you, dude." Graham claps me on the back.

The three of them take off in the opposite direction toward the parking lot, and I shove my bag in the compartment and join Briggs. He's got his AirPods in, gazing out the window, and although I take a seat next to him, I don't say anything. He knows what's at stake, and it's up to him to get it together.

When we get back to the hotel, Briggs goes to his room without saying goodnight and I take the elevator up to my floor. Walking to my door, I slide my key card into the slot. The green light beeps then I let myself inside as quietly as I can.

Shit, I don't realize how late it is until I see the glowing lights of the clock that say it's past midnight. I toe off my shoes and look toward the bed and see Holland wrapped in the plush white blanket. Her honey hair fanned out around her.

She looks like a damn angel swathed in white. Her dark lashes rest on her cheeks that are flushed from the warmth of the room.

A part of me wishes that I was the kind of guy who deserves her. That I could come home from every late-night game and find her here in my bed like she's meant to be there.

Thoughts I shouldn't even be thinking and that definitely don't go with our rules.

When I press my knee into the bed to climb in with her, she stirs sleepily.

"Reed?" Her voice is husky with sleep, and fuck, it shoots straight to my dick.

"Yeah, babe, it's me. How was tonight?"

She sits up on her elbows and looks at the clock. "God, I can't believe I fell asleep. I was trying to wait up for you, but I must have dozed off while I was waiting."

I pull the blanket back and slide into bed with her, pulling her small frame against me.

"I talked to the guys for a little bit, got caught up."

"Mmm." She wiggles against me slightly, causing me to bite my lip in restraint. I don't want to be a dick, but my dick has a thing for Holland and right now she's pressed against it.

Untangling herself from my grip, she turns to face me and gives me a shy smile. "It's kind of weird. Falling asleep in your bed. Don't you think?"

I nod. "I can't say I ever thought this would be a thing, but I'm not mad about it."

She pulls her bottom lip into her mouth, a sultry expression passing over her face. Her chest is rising quickly, the pulse in her neck pounding wildly. The feeling is mutual; Holland wants me just as badly as I want her.

"Been thinking about you all night. I could hardly focus on the damn puck."

Her giggle is sweet. She inches closer until her lips are only a centimeter away from mine. I can feel her warm breath on my lips. So fucking close. I want to kiss those plump lips, then I want to hear my name fall from them like a prayer.

"Have you, Mr. Star Forward, hot shot NHL player?" She breathes, her tongue darting out to wet her lips. I feel her hands sliding down my chest, lower and lower, brushing over my abs that tighten against her touch. Her fingers dip underneath the cotton of my t-shirt to run against the bare skin above my waistband.

It makes me fucking shiver. I don't know what this girl is doing to me, but everything she does drives me insane and now I want my hands on her. I can't wait a second longer.

I lace my hands in her hair and yank her toward me until she collides with my lips, then roll until she's beneath me. Her hands fist into my shirt, pulling me closer.

It's not close enough. I want more. I need more with Holland. The irony of what this feels like isn't lost on me. Instead, I kiss her harder, snaking my hands under the satin of her camisole until my finger brushes over the hard peak of her nipple. Her skin is as silky as the fabric of her shirt, and I want to run my tongue along the dips and valleys of her skin.

I use both hands to pull it over her head and then toss it to the side, leaving her naked from the waist up under me. The room is dark, with only the dim neon glow of the tv, but I can still make out the shape of her. She's perfect. Everything a man could want in a woman. Her curves are perfect for my hands, and I'll never tire of trying to memorize every inch of her.

There's not enough time in the world to get my fill.

I'm always going to be starving for more.

I wrench my lips from hers and kiss down her neck, sucking on the spot that makes her pant my name, then move lower and lower until I can give attention to the needy hardened peaks. Rosy and pink, they seem to flush with her, standing out against her pale skin.

Switching from left to right, I suck, bite, and rub my beard along her breasts, scraping the sensitive flesh until she's squirming beneath me. I drag her shorts down her body and she kicks them to the side. They pool at her ankles, leaving her in nothing but a tiny scrap of satin.

I rub my nose along the front of her pussy, inhaling her scent.

God, I love it. I want to bury my face in her pussy and eat her until I have to come up for air. Contrary to popular belief, men love the smell of their girls' pussy, and I plan to give it lots of attention that proves that theory correct.

"Reed," Holland begs, pulling at the long strands of my hair as I kiss her greedy little clit through her panties.

"You need more, baby?" I run my tongue along the seam of her, still on top of her panties. She groans in frustration, and I laugh.

"Mmm, I think you're being a greedy girl, Holland."

I wind the satin in my hand and pull, popping the strings free in one swift motion. Fuck, she's so wet. I toss her panties to the side and take one long lick of her pussy, coating my tongue with her wetness.

Using my thumb, I trace her clit in gentle, teasing circles, driving her mad. I want her this way, wet and soaking, begging for me to slide inside of her to cure the ache.

"Reed, please." She's pleading now. Her voice desperate and edgy, and I fucking love it.

"You want me to make it feel better? Make that ache inside of you go away?"

She nods furiously, arching off the bed when I slide my middle finger inside of her. I rub the spot while I suck her clit into my mouth, and watch as she begins to tighten around my finger. I'll never get tired of seeing her fall apart and cave to the pleasure I bring her.

There's *nothing* like it in the goddamn world.

I pull back and look up at her, only for our eyes to meet in an intense, burning stare. She pulls me back up her body and yanks at my shirt, desperately trying to get it off me. I reach behind my head and pull it off, all while watching her hungry eyes rake down my chest, to my abs then down to where my cock is straining against my grey sweatpants.

"You are the reason women love grey sweatpants." She groans. Her tiny hand reaches out to rub my cock through my pants, and I'm surprised by her boldness. Maybe she's caught up in the moment, but fuck, I love this side of her. She pushes me back onto the bed, hooking her pink nails into my waistband, and pulls my briefs down with my sweats. When my cock pops free, she puts both hands around me, pumping once and then twice, using her thumb to swirl the bead of precum seeping from the slit, causing me to groan out loud.

Holland sits up on her knees and pulls her bottom lip nervously into her mouth, then looks up through her thick, dark lashes. "I want to be on top. Is that... okay?"

I could fucking cry. Is. That. Okay? This woman really just asked me if she could ride my cock.

"Babe, you never have to ask for what you want. Take it."

She looks at me sheepishly, her cheeks flushing red. I don't let her retreat into her head; instead, I pull her back to me, desperate to feel her skin against mine, then bring my lips to hers. I run my hands up her waist then her sides, cupping her tits as she straddles me. The pert little peaks of her nipples stand upright, begging to be sucked. I lean up slightly and capture one between my teeth and tug lightly, causing her to moan.

Everywhere she touches blazes a path and I'm burning for her. Her warm, wet center is nestled against my cock and just another inch, I can slide inside her. She rises up on her knees and I fist my cock, dragging it through her folds. The broad head grinding against her clit. Her sharp intake of breath shows how much she likes that. We stay like that for a few moments, her rocking back and forth, dragging her clit against my cock.

Fuck, she feels incredible. Everything about her. Her scent, her body. I place my hands on her tits and squeeze gently then roll her nipple between my fingers.

One thing I've already learned about Holland is how responsive her nipples are. They're sensitive, and each time I touch them, she seems to inch closer and closer to orgasm, and fuck, I want to see if I can make her come just from sucking and biting them. But, another time. I want her squeezing my cock when she comes this time.

The head of my cock nudges against her entrance, and she places her hands around me to line us up perfectly, and then slowly... so fucking slow, she inches down on me.

For the first time in my life, I swear I see Heaven.

White lights and blinding pleasure have me squeezing her hips to keep from thrusting up to the hilt inside her.

Holy fuck.

"Oh god," she moans, slowly sliding down on me until I'm fully seated inside her.

I'm currently reciting the alphabet in my head in order to not come. I was not prepared for how tight or how fucking perfect she would feel wrapped around me, and now I feel like a teenager.

My eyes fly open to look at her above me. Her blonde hair falls in a curtain over her face as she begins to ride me, rising up then slamming herself back down on my cock.

"Holland," I grunt, reaching up to push her hair back from her face so I can see how beautiful she is.

Her dark ocean eyes drag up to meet mine. This feels unlike anything I've ever experienced. It feels like more than sex. More than two people trying to get each other off. When she slams back down on my cock, and my head nudges against the deepest part of her, I slide my hands around her back and flip us over in one swift motion. Now, she's underneath me, and I'm putting her leg on my shoulder, so I can fuck her like I've been dying to since the first night I touched her. My hips slam into her, hard thrusts that send her farther up on the bed. I rub my thumb along her clit with each thrust and she palms her breasts, pulling at her nipples.

Seeing her touch herself is almost enough to cause me to spill inside of her, but I won't without her.

"I want you to come on my cock, Holland. That's it, baby," I quicken my thumb against her clit, "milk my cock."

"I'm coming," she breathes. I lean forward and capture her lips, just as she squeezes my cock, exploding around me. She moans into my mouth, as her body shakes, and her hips tremble with the power of her orgasm.

Seconds later, I thrust deep and let go, coming inside of her. I can't fucking move as my entire body is overcome with ecstasy. Nothing in the world has ever felt like Holland does wrapped around me, and I don't think anything ever will again.

I'm ruined.

Her nails drag up my back, causing me to hiss, and I drop my forehead down to hers. Words escape me.

What do you say to the girl who just ruined you for anyone else?

"Wow." She breathes, giggling.

I roll to my side, still inside of her, even though I'm starting to soften. I'm not ready to let her go. To let this entire moment go. Pulling her to my chest, I wrap my arms around her small body and she snuggles into the crook of my neck. We're both a sweaty, sticky mess. And then I realize why we're both as sticky as we are.

"Fuck, Holland.... the condom."

"Um, I'm on birth control. I haven't been with anyone in a long time, way before my last check."

I drop my lips to her hair, and wish that hearing that didn't sound so damn good. "I get checked regularly for the team. If you're okay with not using them, then I'm okay."

"I'm okay. I trust you, Reed."

We lie there in comfortable silence, still wrapped in each other with no intention of moving, and after a few minutes, I feel Holland go slack in my arms and her breathing even out.

She's fallen asleep. Another first for me. I've never done this before either. Cuddled, slept with a woman, and I can't imagine it being anyone other than Holland.

Now I realize why she wanted to put these rules in place to begin with, only I'm already dangerously close to breaking them.

CHAPTER THIRTEEN
HOLLAND

Reed: Octopuses are carnivores, they only eat meat. Did you know that?

"Why are you smiling like that?"

I look up quickly, locking my phone and shoving it back into the pocket of my hoodie.

"Nothing, I saw something funny on Facebook."

Emery looks like she doesn't believe me whatsoever, but doesn't press. We're on her couch binge-watching *One Tree Hill* on Netflix and eating way too many carbs for one sitting, but we're celebrating.

"I can't believe I passed that exam. I thought for sure I was going to bomb it. When I sat down in my chair, I was so nervous that my legs were sweating. Whose legs sweat when they're nervous?"

She shrugs, popping another Skittle into her mouth. "Who cares, you rocked that shit, and now you can relax and stop giving me second-hand anxiety."

My laugh is loud and obnoxious but so is that statement. "You?

Imagine how I felt. It was sixty percent of my grade. If I failed it, I would've had to retake that entire class. The. Entire. Class. Em."

"But you didn't. You passed because you're a badass bitch, and we don't have time for negative energy in our lives."

"Preach."

I grin, despite the fact that my troubles are far from over, I'm going to enjoy my moment of celebration with my best friend. The exam was yesterday and the professor just posted our results today, so I called Em and said we should celebrate.

When I texted Reed to let him know I passed, he recorded a video of him and Evan congratulating me, which made me a pile of goo on the floor. That man is too handsome and too ridiculously charming for his own good.

"You know what?" Em says, sitting up from the couch, "let's go out. We need drinks, we need to shake our asses, and we need to celebrate the fact that you're basically a functioning adult in society."

"Or, we could stay in and binge watch *The Vampire Diaries*."

"We can do that any night of the week, but what we can't do is tequila shots at a bar while you're still on your celebration high." She stands from the couch and looks at me with pleading eyes. "Please? I have this new leather skirt that I've been dying to wear. It's boring when you're not here."

Guilt creeps up my chest at the mention of my absence, which then causes me to think about Reed, and feel even more guilty for what I've been doing. I hate keeping things from her. I hate that I have to hide what's making me happy, but holding onto our friendship is more important to me.

"Okay, fine. But I get to wear the burgundy dress."

She doesn't hesitate. "Done! I'm going to shower. Brb."

Once she's left the room, I pull my phone out and open to Reed's message, then type a quick response.

Me: More random octopus facts, watching documentaries with Ev again?

The bubble pops up, signaling his response.

Reed: Nah, just wanted an excuse to text you ;)

Those stupid butterflies swirl in my stomach again. I bite my lip, debating on how to respond. He's obviously flirting, but I shouldn't read too much into it, right?

Should I respond with something flirty back, or just keep it casual?

Okay, non-relationships are hard. Where's the 'How to' book for this?

Me: Not that you need an excuse, but hi. What are you guys up to?

Reed: We've been playing a very intense game of castle building for the last hour, and now he's talked me into going to the aquarium tomorrow to see live octopuses. Wanna come?

My heart flips in my chest. Partially from the thought of spending more time with Reed, but more so of the fact that I don't know how to explain that to Em. Would she even ask?

Me: Is that a good idea?

Reed: I'm a rule breaker, babe, gonna have to get used to it.

141

Reed: Plus, Evan specifically asked for Ollie to come, so...

Me: Fine. Only because Evan asked and I know he's going to be so excited to see an octopus in person.

Reed: He's going to Ma's for a sleepover, so... I'll pick you up at eight in the morning?

Me: Thumbs up emoji with a kissy face

Perks of living next door to his mom and Emery, I guess. I think to myself.

I swipe the message away and set my phone down on the table before going to Emery's room to start getting ready. Now, I just have to make it through tonight.

"Don't kill me."

Three words you don't want to hear when your best friend drags you to a bar after midnight and all you want to do is be at home in your pajamas stuffing your face.

My eyes narrow. "Okayyyyy." I drag the last syllable out, already suspicious of what's about to come out of her mouth.

"Uh, so remember that guy I told you about? The paralegal I went out with?" Emery says, squinting her nose. "And the guy I said I was going to hook you up with?"

Oh no, I don't like where this is going. Not at all.

"Well, they were in the neighborhood, so they're going to stop by."

"Emery," I groan, "no. Please do not do this to me tonight. We're celebrating remember?"

I hold up my drink and shake the ice around, wishing I hadn't agreed to come out tonight in the first place. But, I miss Em. I miss being able to spend every day with her and make charcuterie boards and binge watch trashy tv.

"It'll be fine. It's almost like fate, right?"

"Except you texted them and told them we were here, Em. I do not want you to try and matchmake me with this guy." My eyes roll. I fold my arms across my chest, suddenly more self-conscious of tonight's outfit choice. If I would've known she was going to trap me in a blind date, I would have worn something more conservative. Less Emery, more me. This is what I get for trying to be brazen and live in the moment.

Emery sips on her mojito. "Babe, you're stressing. Don't. It's a total laid back, no pressure kind of thing. Now drink up and get your sweet ass on the dance floor so we can shake it."

There's no sense in arguing with her. She means well, she does. I know she has a heart of gold. We're just complete and total opposites, and honestly, looking at the two of us, you'd think we would never be friends. She's always been the fun, outgoing, energetic one of our friendship, with me being the shy and reserved one. When we go to parties or anything social, Em is the one that never meets a stranger. The kind of person you're drawn to. She has this ability to make anyone feel comfortable. A gift I definitely do not possess.

I finish off my drink and set it on the table before standing shakily on the heels she insisted I wear.

"You have got to wear these; they make your legs look even hotter with that dress."

Me: Remind me to never let Emery talk me into anything, literally ever again.

I send the message to Reed before I can change my mind then tuck my phone back into my purse just as Emery walks up. And she's not alone. There's a tall guy who looks like he probably has more fashion sense than I do, wearing a crisp polo tucked into slacks with a black sports jacket.

Country club, Range Rover driving, golf on the weekends, frat boy alumni.

Totally Emery's type.

Love her to death, but the girl has a type.

He's got dark eyes and a kind smile. Even though I didn't want to meet anyone tonight, I get a good vibe from him.

"Hi, I'm Landon. I work with Emery. Holland, I'm assuming?"

He holds out his hand, and I shake it quickly then nod. "I am. Nice to meet you."

Then I drag my eyes to the guy next to him: my "blind date" for the night. He's a little shorter than Landon, and his complete opposite. Almost like Emery and me. His blond hair is messy and sticking up in every direction, and he's wearing a pair of dark jeans and a white t-shirt. Simple, but put-together.

He smiles, and I see he's got dimples on both his cheeks.

"And you must be the infamous Holland," he teases. "I'm Aaron. Best friends with this douchebag, but don't hold it against me."

I laugh. "Yes, I'm Holland."

Emery grins and loops her arm in Landon's. "You owe me a dance for filing your five mountains of paperwork Friday. Let's go."

I almost feel for the guy, his pained expression is evident before she drags him off to the middle of the dance floor, leaving Aaron and me alone.

"Not gonna lie, had no idea he was dragging me here tonight." Aaron laughs. He signals for the bartender, then orders a beer, and turns to me. "Can I get you a drink?"

"Sure. Manhattan, please."

He nods and tells the bartender. I feel my phone vibrate in my purse, so I slip it out and quickly check my messages.

Reed: Do I even want to know?

Me: Your sister trapped me into a blind date.

He immediately responds.

Reed: Where are you?

Me: Downtown, SoHo bar. Don't worry, I'm keeping an eye on her ;)

The typing bubble appears, then disappears, then appears again. Is he deciding what to respond?

I wait for his reply, but he doesn't, so I put my phone away.

Aaron slides me my drink with a smile. "So, Emery said you're in school to be a librarian. That's amazing. Where do you think you'll work once you graduate?

School is safe territory. The last thing I want to do is give him the wrong impression, but I guess casual conversation wouldn't hurt.

"I'd really like to work at a university. Ideally. But, wherever I end up, if there are books then I'll be happy."

We walk over to an empty table off to the side of the dance floor, that's quieter, and sit down.

"Sometimes I think I have it all figured out, and the next minute, everything changes," I say. "I think once I graduate, I'll have a better feel of things.

Aaron nods. "I get what you mean. I'm in my third year of med school, and I start my residency soon. Sometimes I want to be in pediatrics, sometimes I want to be in obstetrics, and other times, I want to be a surgeon."

"Life decisions are hard."

We spend the next thirty minutes chatting, and I realize that while I'm not interested in Aaron romantically, he would be an awesome friend. We have a lot in common and talking to him has been easy, like we've always known each other. Honestly, I get the vibe that he may swing for the other team, but he didn't bring it up, and I wasn't going to pry. I'm fine just talking with him.

"Wanna dance?"

"I have two left feet. Seriously, it's terrible." I laugh, shaking my head.

He stands and extends his hand. "Do me the honor, librarian Holland, and let me have this dance."

A slow tune plays through the speakers. I roll my eyes and laugh before placing my hand in his as he leads us to the dance floor. He pulls me to him, and I lace my hands around his neck.

And even though we're pressed together on a dance floor, it feels strictly platonic, like dancing with a cousin. I smile up at him, awkwardly.

God, Holland, that's terrible. You're supposed to be on a blind date and you're thinking of the guy as your distant cousin.

This is why you'll be single forever.

"Alright, moment of honesty, I *hate* this song," he mutters, and I throw my head back and laugh.

Out of the corner of my eye, I see someone approaching us, and when I look up, I see Reed. He's standing right next to me, looking ridiculously handsome in the low club lighting.

Wait, why is he here?

"Reed?" I ask, my jaw hanging down. "What are you doing here?"

He clenches his jaw, then forces a fake smile on his face. "Texted Em and she said you guys were here, and Evan's with Ma for the night, so I figured I would come out."

Aaron looks at him in confusion. "Okay... uh, we're dancing, do you mind?"

Reed looks at him then back at me. "Actually, I do. Why don't you take a fucking hi-"

"Annnnnnd, I will be right back. Sorry," I apologize to Aaron, removing my arms from around his neck. I grab Reed by the arm and drag him off the dance floor. He's like steel beneath my touch, all amped up, and I have no idea what the hell is happening right now.

I take him down the dark hallway, past the bathrooms, until we're at the back door and then I push it open, stepping outside. Once it shuts behind us, and it's just the two of us, I let him have it.

"What the hell was that, Reed Davidson?" I screech.

My heart is pounding in my chest. I'm embarrassed by how he just acted, but also a little turned on, because Reed was jealous. He was so jealous of Aaron that he couldn't stand it.

"What do you mean, what was that, Holl? He had his fucking hands on you, almost touching your ass."

Reed throws his hands in the air then runs them frustratedly through his mess of brown curls. He paces back and forth in front of me.

"You can't just bust in somewhere and demand someone not touch me. That's not how things work, Reed."

He stops pacing and looks at me; there's fire in his eyes as he steps closer. "You think I don't know that? You think I don't know that I have no right to be jealous? No right to feel so fucking possessive over you like you're mine."

"You're right. Because we made rules. Rules to protect both of our hearts, and this doesn't fit in them, Reed."

Stepping closer, he slides his hands up my jaw, cradling it, tenderly. Gently. "I'm sorry, Holl. I just... I lost my fucking head in there. I'm sorry."

I nod and hold his hands at my jaw. "You can't do that again. No one can know. Remember?" I say our second rule out loud, and it feels bitter against my tongue."

Reed sighs heavily, then drops his forehead to mine. "Can you do me a favor and not touch him while I'm here? It guts me, Holland."

"Yes. It was innocent, Reed, he's a good guy. We were just talking and he asked me to dance, so I said sure."

"I just... I lost my head, Holland. I couldn't stand to see his hands on you. Even if it was innocent, my damn blood is boiling."

"I think I'm going to go home. I'm exhausted, and Em has been with Landon all night, so it's not like she's going to miss me."

His brow furrows. "Does that mean you'll come home with me?"

I bite my bottom lip, debating on whether or not I should. "After that caveman act you pulled inside? I don't know, Reed. Maybe I should just go home alone."

Cutting my eyes at him, playfully, I pull his hands from my face and take a step back. My heels click against the pavement as I put some much-needed space between us.

Reed's gaze darkens. "Are you... playing hard to get, Holland Parker?"

I give him the most sultry, pouty look I can then shrug.

"I will throw your ass over my shoulder and carry you all the way back to my house, don't bite off more than you can chew, babe."

Babe.

I never realized how much I loved that word until it came from Reed's lips.

"Hmmm..."

Before I can take another step back, Reed is stalking forward. He grabs me around the waist and pulls me to him before leaning down to kiss me breathless. His tongue tangles with mine until we're both panting. The way my body responds to Reed; it's never been this way for me, not with anyone else. Like I was made just for him and he's the only one who can make me feel so alive.

I've missed him, and even though I can't admit it out loud, I was dying for this. For him.

"Take me home, Reed."

He grins, then squats down and hoists me over his shoulder, in true caveman fashion.

"Oh my god, Reed, put me down!" I screech. "Someone's going to see my butt in this dress!"

If that happens, I'll be mortified and die. Death by embarrassment. It's an actual thing, look it up. Thank God we're in a dark alley and alone, or I might actually have to kill him.

I feel a sharp sting on my ass from Reed's hand as he slaps it. Hard.

Well... I guess that's my answer.

CHAPTER FOURTEEN

REED

I lost my head tonight. Hearing Holland tell me she was on a blind date with that douchebag, I left all rational thought at home when I showed up at that club. Fuck, I don't know what I thought I was going to do by going there or what I thought I would accomplish, but that's the point. I didn't think.

Just imagining his hands on her, it drove me fucking *insane*. I don't think I've ever felt like that about a woman, on the brink of insanity, just at the thought of someone else touching her. Fuck, even just looking at her.

The thought still makes me want to put my fist through something. The problem with all of this, me being jealous or possessive over Holland, is that it isn't in our rules.

"I'm still mad at you," Holland mutters grumpily, but her words lack conviction. She's laid out on my bed, wearing one of my t-shirts that hangs down to her thighs. Her face is bare, her hair is in a messy knot on the top of her head, and honestly, I've never seen her more beautiful.

There's something about seeing her in *my* clothes that makes me dizzy with lust. Maybe it's the possessiveness I feel inside of me tonight. I want to see her in nothing but my shirt from here on out and I'll be happy. After the club, we came home and got ready for bed, and I gave her space. I didn't want to push it after what happened. I took a quick shower, brushed my teeth and threw on an old pair of sweats while I waited for her to finish in the guest bathroom.

"I'm sorry, babe, can I make it up to you?" I grin. I am sorry that I acted the way I did, and I don't have an excuse for it, except that she makes me crazy.

"Hmmm." She bites her lip and pretends to think on the idea.

Instead of waiting for her answer, I drop to the floor in front of her and grasp her hips, pulling her to the end of the bed. She squeals as I nip at the inside of her thigh.

"I have an idea of exactly how I'm going to make it better." I pull her panties down her hips, dragging them down her thighs. Her pretty, rosy pussy glistens, waiting for me to make it stop aching. "How about this?" I take a long, slow lick of her from her opening to her clit, then nibble on the greedy little nub.

The soft skin of her thighs is red and angry from my beard brushing against it. The idea that I've marked her in some way makes me even harder.

"Reed," she moans, threading her fingers in my hair and yanking when I take lazy swipes, "more."

"I love when you get bossy." I grin against her pussy before pulling back to look up at her. "Touch yourself."

She looks at me like I'm crazy. "What? Don't stop."

"I want you to touch yourself, and I want to watch." I pull her fingers down to her pussy, over her clit. "You know how many times I've fantasized about this since I picked you up from that sorority house? How many times I've come on my fucking fist dreaming about watching you make yourself come with my name on your lips."

Holland bites her lip nervously, but doesn't remove her hand. "Only... Only if you make yourself come too."

My shy girl. She's so damn sweet. I'm addicted to her. Every goddamn part.

I yank my sweats down then free my straining cock from the confines of my briefs. Holland's gaze narrows, her eyes zeroing in on my fist, and her little pink tongue darts out to wet her lips.

"Rub your clit. Slow, light circles. Like my tongue is flicking over it," I tell her.

Her gaze darkens, but she does as she's told. Using two fingers, she works her clit slowly, holding my eyes.

"Good girl," I say hoarsely, "keep going."

I fist my cock, pumping it in sync with her hand. Slow strokes. When Holland's hand speeds up and her breath quickens, I can tell she's close, so I step forward and drag my cock through her folds, coating myself with her slickness.

"You're dripping all over me, baby, did you like that? Me watching you? Telling you what I wanted you to do?"

She nods.

"On your knees."

At first I was worried she wouldn't want things to be like this between us, but her body tells me everything I need to know. Holland loves this shit, just as much as I do, and I hope her trust in me allows me to take her body to a new place. So that when this "arrangement" is over, she'll remember me. Remember that no one can bring her the pleasure that I can.

Holland flips over, tossing her long blonde hair over her shoulder to look back at me. I spread her knees and glide my hand from her ass, up the base of her spine, all the way to the back of her neck, where I push her slightly forward onto the bed. Her cheek's pressed against the mattress, and she looks back at me with a small smirk.

With one hand on the back of her neck, one hand grasping the soft flesh of her hips, I grind my cock against her center. She greedily pushes back against me, trying to create friction to ease the ache.

Don't worry, baby, I'll give you what you want. We're both on edge, even more so after the show she put on, and I can't wait to sink inside of her. After tonight, I have so many thoughts roaring through my head, ones that I can't seem to ignore. The possessive, caveman kind that tell me to claim Holland as mine, even though I know that can't happen.

I line my cock up with her entrance and push inside, slowly, savoring the feel of how wet and tight she is wrapped around me as I ease into her body.

Being with Holland is bliss. I'm convinced her body was made just for me. My hips surge forward until I'm buried inside of her. So deep, I don't know where she starts and I end, and it's fucking heaven.

Her tiny hands are fisted in the sheets, and each time I withdraw and slam back into her tight body, they squeeze until her knuckles are white from how hard she's grasping them.

"Reed, more, please," she pleads.

My hands grip her waist harder as I power into her, my thrusts brutal and deeper each time. I reach down between us to rub her clit. I need to get her there, need her to fall apart on my cock. Every time my hips slap against her ass, white hot pleasure shoots down my spine.

"Come, Holland, come on my cock," I whisper hoarsely. I can't last another fucking second with her squeezing my cock this way and I can't go unless she's with me.

A few more rough swipes of my thumb, and she's moaning my name. The sweetest sound in the goddamn world, exploding around me. Her pussy tightens, and that's all it takes to send me over the edge. I fall with her, burying myself deep and coming inside of her. I come so hard that black spots cloud my vision. I lean forward, my body folding over hers, and kiss a path up her spine. Fuck, I can feel us spilling from her, and it's the hottest thing I've ever felt.

I've never been with anyone without protection. Another first with Holland.

She sways slightly, so I pull out of her gently, then sit back to look at her. I can't help it. The sight of my cum sliding out of her is almost enough to make me hard again.

This girl has fucking ruined me. Without a doubt.

I get up, walk to the bathroom and grab a rag. After wetting it with warm water, I join her back on the bed and gently clean her up. She sighs contently and cuddles into the covers. I toss the rag into the laundry bin and pull the covers over us, sliding in next to her.

I wrap her in my arms, and she burrows into the crook of my neck, her fingers absentmindedly fingering my beard.

"I have to pick Evan up tomorrow afternoon, but I want to take you somewhere in the morning. We're rescheduling the aquarium so Emery can be there whYou down?" I ask.

Holland looks up at me with sleepy, sated eyes and nods. "Where?"

I smirk. "Wouldn't be a surprise if I told you, would it?"

"Just as long as I can sleep past eight. I haven't slept in, in so long."

Leaning down, I kiss her, soft and sweet. "Get some sleep, babe. I'll go for a run in the morning, and I won't wake you."

She murmurs sleepily, but the next thing I know, she's snoring. A light, cute as fuck snore, and I laugh. Holland Parker is wrecking me, and I have no intention of stopping it.

I can't remember the last time I slept so peacefully. I didn't wake up once until the sunlight streamed into the windows in my bedroom. Usually, I'm up before the sun and get a run or a workout in with a protein shake. Today, I slept in with Holland and I don't regret a single second of it. She's fast asleep in my arms, tucked tightly against my body.

The morning sun casts a warm, orange glow on her already perfect skin. I stay like this, propped up on my elbow, watching the steady rise and fall of her chest as she sleeps. Her dark lashes fanned out on her cheeks, her pouty, plump rose-colored lips completely free of makeup. Her skin is flawless, and she's beautiful. I could watch her sleep all day, but I want to take her somewhere today and I don't have long to do it.

My lips brush against the warm, sun-kissed skin of her shoulder. After a few times, she begins to stir, a sleepy groan leaving her lush lips.

"Good morning, beautiful," I say, my hands sliding tighter around her stomach.

"Mmm, good morning."

She looks back over her shoulder at me and gives me a sleepy smile.

"Did you sleep well?"

"Yes. This bed is amazing. I could sleep here every night, it's like a cloud."

I could too, I think, but keep the thought to myself. She asked for casual, but every day I find it harder and harder to be anything but all-in.

"I'm going to go make a smoothie and take a quick shower. I want to leave in the next hour. Think we can make it happen?" I ask.

She nods against my arm, but makes no move to get up.

I laugh and kiss her behind the ear. "Get that sweet ass up."

"I'm sorry, this bed. It's heavenly."

The bed has nothing to do with how much I want to stay, and everything to do with the girl in it.

After a quick shower, I throw on some jeans and a tee and make us both smoothies for the road. I sit down at the bar and text Mom to check on Evan. She sends a photo of the two of them making pancakes and I smile.

God, I love that kid.

"All ready."

I look up and see Holland standing in front of me in a sweater and a pair of jeans with knee-high black boots. She looks good enough to eat.

"Reed..." she warns, with a smirk, "if you keep looking at me like that, we're never going to this secret place you keep telling me about."

"Fine. I can't help that I want to bring you right back to bed and pick up where we left off last night."

Her cheeks redden, and I grin. "I love that I make you blush. C'mon, let's go."

I hold out my hand for her, and she slides her small one into mine. We walk to the truck and I help her inside since she's so fucking tiny then I pull out onto the highway. Holland has no idea where I'm taking her, but I've been thinking about it for a while and doing research, so having a few days off is the perfect time to bring her.

We drive for thirty minutes, out of the city and into the country part of Illinois. Finally, I pull my truck into the long gravel road, and Holland looks at me in confusion.

"Serenity Ranch? What is this?"

I keep driving, but take her hand in mine. "You'll see."

She looks nervous, but when I squeeze her hand to reassure her, she smiles at me.

This place is beautiful. Nestled on the outskirts of Chicago, it's a piece of heaven all in itself. Acres and acres of farmland with rolling green hills, tall tree lines, and fresh air.

When I park and help Holland out, the owner, Bert, walks over and greets us. I've spoken to him a few times on the phone in the past few weeks and recognized his picture from the website's directory.

"Mr. Davidson?" he asks. Tall, wiry, with a kind smile and a cowboy hat, Bert immediately gives off a good vibe. He seems trustworthy and genuine based on the conversations that we have had.

I stick my hand out for him to shake. "Hi, yes. Call me, Reed, this is my girl-... This is Holland." Shit. Holland looks at me with wide eyes, then smiles and shakes Bert's hand.

"So Holland, welcome to Serenity Ranch. I've been speaking with Reed for a few weeks now about our program, and I know he wanted to surprise you."

Holland looks at me then back at Bert. He just smiles warmly and gestures for us to walk with him.

"My wife Delores and I started Serenity Ranch ten years ago now. My father-in-law was diagnosed with Alzheimer's, and my wife decided to buy this little slice of heaven, and dedicate our lives to helping others who were diagnosed the same as he was. We've spent the last ten years growing it into what you see today."

Holland's teary, and I know she's starting to understand why I brought her here.

Bert continues walking down the dirt path until we get to a large stable with several horses grazing about.

"We offer a safe place with certified nurses as well as volunteers to give people with Alzheimer's a place where they feel needed. We have animal therapy, gardening, group time, and therapy dogs here on the property. Sometimes people with Alzheimer's just need a place where they feel unrestricted by everyone, that's also safe. That is the goal here at Serenity Ranch."

She gazes out at the farm, the large barn and the animals. "This place is incredible, Bert. What you and your wife are doing, it's amazing."

I grab Holland's hand and squeeze it gently in mine and she looks up at me. Her blue eyes are swimming with tears. "Thank you," she mouths.

"Bert, could you give us a second?"

"Absolutely. I'll be right over here if you guys need anything."

When it's just the two of us, I pull her to me, and tip her chin up so I can gaze into her eyes. "I hope I wasn't overstepping by finding this place. I just… after seeing your dad, I wanted to see what this place was about. A buddy of mine, his mom has Alzheimer's, and she comes here a lot. He said that he thinks it has truly made her happier. What if your dad came here, baby?"

A tear slips free from her eye, and I swipe it away. "Reed, this place probably costs a fortune, but God, it's amazing. I want to know more about it, but just what I've seen, it looks incredible. This could be life-changing for him."

I nod. "That's why I wanted to surprise you with this. Holland, I've known your dad longer than I've known my own. He was there for me whenever I didn't have a father. He's important to me, and if I could do this for him, if you'd allow me to take care of this, it would mean a lot to me."

Holland's fully crying now. A sob escapes her lips and I swallow it in a deep kiss that I feel down to my soul.

"That would be the most amazing thing anyone has ever done for our family, Reed," she whispers.

"Let's tour the rest of the place and meet some of the staff, and if you want him to come here, I'll pay for the year up front."

Holland cries quietly the rest of the tour, but gazes at all of the amenities in awe. After Bert has taken us around the entire ranch, I have no doubt in my mind. This place is incredible.

"Here's a brochure for the ranch and my number is on the back. Feel free to call me at any time to discuss. We also have a program that allows for live-in care here at the ranch. I know that's a big step and one that you might not be interested in, but the option is here."

"Thanks for meeting us, Bert. I appreciate the tour." I shake his hand again, and then walk Holland back to the truck. Once we're inside, I face her. "What do you think, babe?"

"I think that he would love it here. You remember how much he loved to do the flower beds?"

I nod. "He was out there, rain or shine, when he wasn't at the mill. Mowed the lawn every other day."

"Thank you, Reed. This means more to me than you'll ever know. I can't explain how... grateful I am."

I pick her hand up and kiss her knuckles. "I just want you to be happy, and I want your dad to be safe and happy in a place that he loves."

"I want to think about it, and talk to his nurses and doctors before we make a decision, maybe after the new year?"

"Whenever you're ready. I'll support anything you decide."

I say it knowing I'd do anything to keep the smile from this afternoon on her face.

CHAPTER FIFTEEN

HOLLAND

Days turn into weeks, fall fades into winter, and during that time, things between Reed and me shift. I didn't say it out loud, but after the ranch, he was different. Not only have things changed between us, but the Avalanche are having their best season ever. They're quickly becoming the highest-ranking team in the NHL, on their way to the Stanley Cup finals, for the second time in two years. Every hockey player's dream.

Reed's dream.

It's been one of the best moments of my life to be front and center, watching it happen. To *feel* Reed's excitement as he wins game after game. His performance is better than ever, and if you ask him? He says that Evan and me are his good luck charms. I know that's just him being Reed, charming as ever, and that it's actually because he's training harder, working smarter, and spending less time partying and more time working on himself.

"Does this dress make me look fat?" Emery asks, modeling her brand-new skintight black mini dress in the mirror of my room.

She's been trying on outfits for the past hour for her company Christmas party that is happening soon at the law firm. She's still going strong with Landon and has been gushing all day about how she wants to impress all of his friends.

"Uh no, but if you bend over, everyone's going to see your Virginia."

She giggles and twirls around in front of the mirror. "So, it's a yes then?"

I raise my eyebrows, and just as I'm about to tell her *absolutely not*, the doorbell rings.

"Okay, don't make any rash decisions. I'll be right back."

Laughing, I walk out of the bedroom and through the foyer to the front door and open it.

A tall guy, holding a box, is standing on the doorstep, and I'm immediately confused.

"Hi, Ms. Parker?"

"Yes, that's me."

He hands me a clipboard with a pen while juggling the box. "I have a delivery for you. Can you sign here, stating you received it?"

I quickly scrawl a messy signature and hand it back to him. He hands me the box, and then says a quick goodbye while I shut the door.

A delivery? From who? I'm not expecting anything.

Carrying the box back into my room, I set it on my dresser and untie the large, red ribbon. I pull the lid off and carefully pull back the white tissue paper. Under the paper is a jersey with the name

DAVIDSON on the back, and a note.

I pick the paper up and read the messy scrawl in black ink.

Beautiful,

Just a little something to show you I was thinking of you. Miss you. Do me a favor and send me a picture of you wearing nothing but this.

;) Reed

"What's that?" Emery's voice comes from right behind me, startling me so badly that the note falls from my hand and goes behind the dresser.

I slam the lid of the box shut then turn around and squeak, "No one. Nothing." I laugh nervously, then realize how suspect that probably looks. I am so not good at this lying to my best friend thing.

"Okaaaay," she says, shaking her head. She turns back toward the mirror. "What about this one?"

The black mini is gone, replaced by a burgundy velvet wrap dress.

My entire body visibly relaxes when I see that she's moved on, and isn't going to force me to show her. What was Reed thinking?

This could've gone so badly.

"Yes, definitely. This is the one. It looks like it was made just for you, Em."

Her face lights up. "Really?" She spins back toward the mirror and runs her hands down the front of the dress.

"Really. Actually, I'm jealous. You're going to have a blast, and you'll be the most beautiful girl in the entire room."

I wasn't lying. Emery has the kind of beauty that when she enters the room, everyone looks. Every head turns. And she never notices. She never sees the attention that she draws, and that's what makes her so beautiful, inside and out.

"I'm nervous, Holl. This is the first time I've ever liked someone this way. You know, something that's not just shallow and "fun." He likes me for who I am, and doesn't expect me to be any different."

"Follow your heart, it won't lead you astray. My dad used to tell me that when we were growing up. I never realized, until I got older, how true that advice is."

I sit down on the edge of the bed and draw my legs up to my chest. Emery walks over and sits down next to me.

"It's scary. Putting yourself out there. All of your flaws, and your quirks, and your cellulite. This is why I don't date." She sighs and falls back on the bed. "After cheating asshole, I'm condemning everyone to the same fate."

I laugh. "You're getting too far ahead of yourself, sister. It is scary to give someone else that power over you, but give him a chance to prove whether he's worthy or not before you start planning the breakup. Not everyone is a cheater, there are plenty of faithful guys out there."

"You're right. This calls for margaritas. Or we could skip the margarita part and head straight for tequila."

"I can't. I have to study for my last midterm. Can you believe that in five months, I'll be graduating and finally have my degree?"

She sits up on her elbows and looks at me. "Yes, I can. Duh.

You've worked hard for this, Holland, you deserve it."

"We are sappy." Laughing, I nudge her with my foot. "This is the dress. Now, I have to get back to studying, but I love you and I'll call you tomorrow?"

"Fine, fine, I'm gone. Call me when you're done and we can go to Starbs and discuss the latest on *The Vampire Diaries*."

"Deal."

After Em leaves, I lie back on my bed with my books and attempt to get work done on my thesis. Except the entire time I'm trying to focus, my eyes keep drifting back to the white box on my dresser.

I bite my lip, trying to focus on the words on my paper, but they're running together. Instead, I'm thinking of the jersey Reed sent and wondering if he actually expects me to send him a picture of me in it.

Probably not.

But... Can you imagine his face if I do?

That's when I decide to do it. To go for it. To do the one thing Reed Davidson least expects me to do.

Pushing my books to the side, I climb off the bed and retrieve the jersey from the box, quickly changing into it. I walk over to the mirror and study my reflection. The blue and white jersey is a size too big, falling over my butt, except for the very bottom where a hint of cheek peeks out, just as if I was wearing a pair of boy shorts.

Satisfied, I walk over to the bed and pick up my phone, snapping a couple of selfies with a pouty lip and then a smile before taking one of the back of the jersey in the mirror with his name and a tease.

Before I can talk myself out of it, I send them. Then try to forget what I just did. I go back to studying while I wait for his reply, and a few minutes later, my phone vibrates.

Reed: Are you trying to kill me? Babe, holy shit... I'm at practice with the guys and this is not the time for a boner.

I grin.

Me: Sorry... not sorry. Didn't think I'd do it, did ya?

Reed: Good thing practice is almost over. Can I swing by? I'll bring dinner.

Me: I have to study. Like actually study, Reed. Not your version where you end up doing something that distracts me and I never finish.

Reed: I'll keep my hands to myself. I promise.

I roll my eyes at his message. We both know that will never happen, but I agree anyway because I miss him.

Me: I have my doubts. See you soon.

Instead of changing back into my old t-shirt and sweats, I leave on his jersey, even though I know it'll be impossible for him to behave and keep his hands to himself. I keep working on my thesis until I hear a soft knock on the door. Grabbing a pair of shorts from my dresser, I quickly slide them on then open the door.

Reed's standing on the doorstep with a bag of food from my favorite restaurant, and my heart dips. Our rules don't specify doing nice things for the other, but they do say no falling in love, and I am hopelessly failing. Every single day my feelings for Reed grow stronger and stronger, breaking each and every one of the rules we set. I'll never tell him, not just because I know he won't feel the same, but because I promised not to be a complication in his life, and love complicates things.

He needs to focus on Evan and his hockey career. Not to mention, I'll lose Emery if she finds out I am in love with her brother. There are so many things working against us. Despite all of that, though, I still wish things were different.

Tonight, he's freshly showered. His messy curls are disheveled as always, and he's wearing a pair of light wash jeans with a black Henley. As always, the butterflies in my stomach seem to explode the second his gaze lands on mine. His eyes travel down my body and a smirk forms on his lips.

"Even better in person."

My stomach dips at the raspy tone of his voice. "Come in." I hold the door open for him to pass through.

"Your dad asleep?"

I nod. "He had a rough day today so he went to bed early."

Reed sets the bag of takeout down on the sofa table then walks over and pulls me to him. "I fucking can't stop thinking about you."

He leans down and presses his lips against mine. His hands, strong and calloused, hold my back, pressing me to him.

Before things get carried away, I pull my lips from his and take a step back. "You said you'd behave."

Shrugging sheepishly, he laughs. "I said I would try. I did."

"Now let me feed you."

That I am not going to argue with. I've been neglecting myself and I'm starving. Aside from Em's visit earlier, and making Dad supper, I've been locked away all day, trying to make headway on my thesis.

I grab the takeout from the table and then Reed's hand, leading him into my room. It's only now that I'm realizing my room is very much still the room I had in high school and I probably should've picked it up before I told him to come by. I set the food down on my nightstand and quickly start to pick up discarded clothes and books that are strewn everywhere.

"I'm sorry it's a mess, I haven't had a chance to clean much yet," I mumble. I shove the clothes in the hamper and put the books on the shelf. I'm flustered, but when Reed walks over and takes a book from my hand, setting it down on the shelf behind me, then takes my chin in his hand, that feeling evaporates.

"Don't care what your room looks like, babe. I'm here for you." He smirks. "And this pizza burrito."

I jab him in the ribs. He leans down and presses a soft, surprisingly chaste kiss to my lips before turning back to the food.

It's a simple moment, but it speaks volumes. About who Reed really is. My fragile heart will never survive this, but I don't want to let him go. Sometimes love can be selfish, and right now, I know that I want to hold on to whatever I have with Reed rather than give him up.

We sit across from each other on my bed and eat dinner, but before we're even done, Reed pushes the food aside and climbs over me then kisses me until we're breathless.

He's a drug, and I can't get enough.

Reed Davidson is the kind of man that you never forget. No matter how much time has passed.

We lie down together on my bed, and Reed flips my bedside lamp off. Above our heads, still glued on the ceiling, are the glow-in-the-dark stars that Emery got me for my sixteenth birthday that still glow just as brightly as the day she gave them to me.

He takes my hand in his and simply holds it. His fingers tightly wound in mine.

This moment between us feels... different. More intimate. The kind of moment that feels monumental, even in the simplicity of it.

"Do you believe in soul mates?" his deep, raspy voice asks.

I look over at him, but can only make out the silhouette of his face in the glow of the fake Milky Way on my ceiling.

"I do. It's fascinating to think somewhere out there in the world, there's someone made just for you. Specifically designed for you."

"Yeah. I've been thinking about it a lot lately. You know my dad left when Emery was a baby."

I nod, and he continues, "I spoke with him for the first time since he left, a few months ago. I haven't stopped thinking about it. About him. And I'm mad at myself for it. For giving him that power over me. I'm angry and I'm fucked up, Holland."

The pain in his voice breaks my heart. Shatters it into tiny shards. I roll toward him and climb over him until I'm lying on top of him. My ear's pressed to his chest while I count the steady thrums of his heartbeat. His hand finds my hair, absentmindedly twirling a loose strand between his fingers.

"I guess the conversation with him made me face shit in my head that I had been tucking away, avoiding. Pretending wasn't really a problem and now I'm facing it. It's not easy, but I think I'm ready to forgive him and I think that it has a lot to do with Evan. He's changed me in the short time he's been here, and I can't imagine going back to how my life was before him. It's like the man upstairs knew that I needed him, even when I didn't know it myself."

"I think that our future is always laid out for us, even before we're ready to see it. Sometimes we're comfortable in our lives and we don't want to see the change that's needed. That's why people are so blindsided when their lives up and change, because they don't want to face the truth. What you're doing is brave, Reed. It's personal growth and that takes courage."

He exhales. His fingers slide into my hair at the nape of my neck as his thumb rubs gentle circles into my scalp. "It doesn't feel like it sometimes, but I think the only way that I can move forward is by forgiving him and letting it go."

I sit up slightly on his chest, and brush a lock of curl off his forehead. It feels like second nature to be this way with Reed. "You can't control other people's actions, but you can control whether or not you let it affect you. I think that dealing with the hurt from him will allow you to move on."

Reed's quiet for a moment. His other hand runs lightly down

my arm, causing goosebumps to erupt on the skin his fingertips brush against. The air in the room feels different, like a shift has happened. I can feel it, and if I had to bet, Reed does too.

"You're a good man, Reed," I whisper in the dark with the stars glowing above us. My eyes grow heavy, exhaustion seeping into my body slowly, until the steady rise and fall of his chest lulls me to sleep.

Just as I'm drifting off, I swear he whispers, "If only a good enough man for you, Holland Parker."

CHAPTER SIXTEEN
REED

❝Weed, can we have a *weal* octopus?" Evan asks me, a genuinely serious expression on his face. Fuck, why are kids so cute? Also, why am I sincerely considering buying him a damn octopus. I bet it would make him smile. This is why they say parents are pushovers because if the kid asked me for a unicorn, I'd do whatever I could to make it happen.

"Bud, octopuses aren't really meant to live in houses with people. They live in the ocean. That's their home."

His brow is furrowed as he thinks about what I've said. "But… what about the aquare-um?"

"Well, that's the exception."

"What's an egg-sep-shun?"

I take a deep breath. "You know, buddy, what if we start with a fish? A little guy like you, and we can name him Pickles two point oh? Maybe one day we can get a real octopus, but for now, I think Pickles will have to do."

"Can it be green?"

I nod. "It can be whatever color you want. We can go pick it out soon, but right now, we have to go because you have a playdate with Ari and Kennedy, and I'm helping Uncle Liam put together some baby thing."

Evan crinkles his nose. "I need to potty."

Here we go. It's go-time. I've been reading book after book about potty training and the different techniques and I've learned enough shit that I know we can do this.

Every child is different, and it's all about what works for them. That I get.

I grab the box of Cheerios from off the top of the pantry and sprint to the bathroom after Evan. He climbs on top of his stool and drops his pants, and before it's go-time, I toss a few Cheerios in the floating water of the toilet bowl then put my fist out.

"You can do it, bud," I say, and his little fist hits mine in a bump.

We're a team, and I'll be damned if we don't tackle this potty journey together.

I turn my back to give him some privacy, and by the heavens above, the sky opens up and low and behold, I hear the sound of a steady stream followed by a cheer.

"I did it, Weed, I did it!"

He jumps up and down and almost falls clean off the stool, but I catch him last minute.

"Bud, I knew you could do it. You realize you're an official big boy now, right?"

The grin on his face is infectious, and I find myself smirking right along with him. It's the first time since he's come to live with me that I feel confident that maybe I can do this. Maybe, somehow, we can figure it out together.

Life is a hell of a lot different than it used to be, but I don't find myself missing those things. I still see Asher, Hudson, Briggs and Graham at practice and, occasionally, we have a beer somewhere, or do a BBQ at someone's house, but fuck, I do not miss wasting my life in a bar. Or chasing after bunnies I have no intention of every seeing again after a one-night stand that left me numb. That's the truth, before Evan... before Holland, I was numb. Numbing myself with girls, partying, drinking, and now, the shit in my life is good, and I don't want to do anything to jeopardize that.

My life's different and I wouldn't want it any other way.

After we pack a quick bag and grab Pickles, we head to Liam's and walk into complete chaos. The second I shut the door behind us, Juliet is running into the foyer. "Hi Reed. Bye Reed!" She runs past me so fast, she slides across the hardwood in her socks.

"Uh, what's going on?" I ask, but she's gone, leaving me and Evan looking at each other like what the hell just happened.

Then Ari and Kennedy come barreling down the hallway, squealing, with Liam on their tales.

"Nerf gun war!" Ari screams, running straight past me, narrowly missing the wall.

Oh. Shit.

We take Nerf wars *very* seriously around here.

"Alright, Ev, we've walked into a battle. Time to prepare." I grab his hand and tug him toward the girls' room, where I snag two guns off the wall. Liam's got Ari and Ken set up with an entire Nerf wall. Shit, I wish I had one of these growing up.

"We don't split up. They're more likely to ambush us if we do. Follow me."

Evan giggles, then slaps his hand over his mouth to silence them. Fuck, he's so cute.

And he's mine, I think.

I tiptoe back into the hallway, holding the plastic gun up like I'm a certified FBI agent about to sweep a house. When I get to the end of the wall, I fly around the corner, checking all the other corners, and find nothing.

"They're sneaky. Never let your guard down."

"What's gu-ard?"

"Never mind. Just follow me, bud."

We need to work on the logistics of war, but we'll get there. He follows me through the house as I search for the girls, and just as I pass by the living room, I hear a giggle. Faint, but definitely Ari.

I point toward the living room, and Evan nods, holding the gun higher. It's about as big as him, and it almost has me dying of laughter, but I manage to keep a straight face while we storm the living room. I spot Ari's plastic high heels poking out from behind the playhouse, so I climb on top of it as quietly as possible, and yell, "Boo."

They scream loud enough to shatter the glass on the windows and crawl out from behind the couch. As soon as Ari's head pops up, Evan pulls the trigger shooting her in the middle of the forehead.

Oh fuck.

Ari's face crumples, and she begins to wail. Poor Evan looks like he's about to start crying right along with her. His panicked gaze darts to mine, and I shake my head. "It's okay, don't worry."

I scoop her up and wrap her in a tight, only kind of hug that Uncle Reed can deliver, and soon, her tears are dry and she's grinning.

"Missed you, Uncle Reed."

"Missed you more, my beauty. I brought a friend for you to play with while I help Daddy and Juliet. This is Evan."

Evan looks up at her with a small, shy smile.

I set Ari down next to him, and Kennedy skips up and pulls Evan in for a strangling hug without pause.

The panicked look returns, and this time I shrug. "Girls, bud. Girls."

Ari looks at the tattered octopus in his hands and asks, "Is this your lovey?"

Evan nods. "His name is Pickles."

"My lovey's name is Princess Sparkles. Want to play in our room?"

He looks at me, and I nod, shooing them out the door. Well... that was easier than expected. But I've realized that kids are resilient like that.

Now that the Nerf war is officially over, I return the guns to the girls' room and make sure they're all set playing before I go upstairs to the spare room that's going to be the new baby's nursery.

The walls are still white, since they've decided to wait to find out the gender, but they've started to fill the room with furniture and gender-neutral decorations.

Juliet's sitting in a white chair in the corner, flipping through the pages of a pregnancy book while Liam is on the floor taking pieces of the baby bed out of the box.

"You guys could have warned me that I was walking into a battlefield."

Juliet laughs. "Where's the fun in that?"

"Just for the record, the guys won. Could've helped your best friend out, man," I tell Liam. He just shakes his head and continues to pull out the wood.

"Alright, dads are on duty." Juliet rises from her recliner and stands. Her pregnant belly is finally starting to show. A little bump beneath her shirt, but Liam still reaches out and rubs it affectionately. "Mama's tired and achy, and I want a bubble bath in complete and total silence."

"I've got dinner and the kids, go relax, baby," Liam coos.

Never seen a guy so in love with his wife. Seeing these two together is the only thing I ever need to believe in love. The real, genuine kind that only comes around once. That's what they share, and man, seeing my best friend be able to experience it after everything he's been through is incredible. No one deserves it like he does.

Juliet gives him a quick kiss then leaves us guys to put together the furniture.

"Still can't believe you guys are waiting to find out the gender until it's time. I need to know."

He laughs. "It's what she wants, and I'm fine doing whatever she wants. Either way, as long as the baby is healthy, that's all that matters to me. Now the girls? They're a different story. They ask us at least twice a day if we'll tell them. Ari tried to bribe me with hugs, but I told her I'm stronger than that."

"I am not surprised."

"So, how are things going with Evan and Holland?"

Shit, right to the good stuff.

"Evan is an awesome kid. I love spending time with him. He peed on the pot-," I stop myself, "toilet today for the first time. It felt like a real victory."

I feel some weird shit in my chest when I think about Ev and the stuff he's overcome just since we met. His nightmares have already slowed down to almost a complete stop now that I got him a nightlight that puts sea figures on the ceiling, and we do, not one, but three stories before bed. He loves anything about the jungle or sea. Big adventures and hell, I love making them up every night to tell him. Not that I can take credit for the nightlight thing. Holland went above and beyond to make a space for Evan where he felt like... Him. Knowing he's obsessed with the ocean and most sea creatures, she made his room into an underwater adventure so that each time he steps foot inside, he looks around in awe.

It didn't really dawn on me how ingrained in our lives Holland has become. We've fallen into a routine that's comfortable and I've gotten used to it.

"Why do you have that look on your face?" Liam asks, brow furrowed in confusion.

"What look? I don't have a look?" I mutter. I'm lying, and judging by the look on his face, he knows it too.

"Don't even. What are you not telling me?"

"Nothing."

Liam throws a bag of screws at me, hitting me right in the face. He picks up a screwdriver next and I throw my hands up in surrender.

"Fine, fuck, fine. This face is the moneymaker, watch it."

"You're an idiot." Liam laughs. "Now tell me what the hell you're hiding. Oh shit, it's Holland, isn't it? That's why you're suddenly being all tight-lipped."

Shit.

"It's complicated."

This time Liam throws his head back and laughs, the deep chuckle echoing off the empty nursery walls.

"Isn't it always? Juliet and I had a complicated thing too and look at us now. Spill."

Sighing, I drag my hand through my unruly mess of hair and look at him. "We set these stupid fucking rules that were supposed to keep things easy. Uncomplicated. Yet, all we did was make a damn mess. And she's perfectly fine with keeping things how they are, but I can't stop thinking about her. It's like every single thing I do, all I can think about is Holland."

"You love her," Liam says simply.

"Woah, that's a very strong word. Too strong. I mean, I don't even know how to love someone."

"Bullshit. You love your ma, Emery, Evan. What about Ari and Kennedy? You have loved them since the day they were born. How about all those times you showed up, Reed? The birthday parties you helped me put together, the days where I had to work late and you picked them up for me?" He pauses, and I can see the sincerity in his eyes. It causes my heart to squeeze, and I'm man enough to admit it. Liam and these girls are as much my family as Ma and Emery, and they always have been. They all give me a purpose in life. Being their uncle. And now... Evan and Holland give me purpose. Just in a terrifying, different way.

"I'm fucking terrified, man. Love? Love is the scariest thing in the damn world. It makes you vulnerable."

"You're right. That's what love does. It splits you open, leaves you raw. It's scary giving someone else the ability to hurt you. But Reed, Juliet is the best thing that ever happened to me, and you know that. She's made me a better man, and I love her so fucking much that I'd do anything in this world for her. Yeah, it was scary to put myself out there and say please love me the way I love you, but if I didn't then I wouldn't have the love of my life, or my family." He stops talking, tearing his gaze from mine and looking down at the baby bed in front of him, then back at me. "Sometimes you just have to push that fear aside and live. You once told me that if I let her walk away, it would be the biggest mistake of my life. Take your own advice."

"She's amazing, and God, I'm crazy about her, but I don't want to hurt Emery. I don't want to ruin the friendship that they share. She'd never forgive me. It's part of the reason we made the stupid rules in the first place."

He shakes his head. "You really think Em is gonna care that you fell in love with her best friend?

"Knowing Em and the fact that she threatened me bodily harm for even looking at Holland, probably. But I think she'd get over it… eventually."

"I think you need to talk to Holland. Tell her how you feel. Be honest. There's nothing wrong with being vulnerable and putting yourself out there."

I nod.

He's right. I need to talk to Holland, and I need to be upfront with her about how these fucking rules aren't working for me anymore.

Not when all I want is to make her mine, and only mine. To have her in my arms every night, to come home to her after days on the road. I fucking love her.

And I have the perfect plan to tell her.

CHAPTER SEVENTEEN
HOLLAND

" Reed," I cry, his long, thick fingers muffling my moans. They're in my mouth after he demanded I suck.

He peeks up at me from between my legs, his unruly dark curls a mess from my constant tugging and pulling while he devours me like a starving man. His eyes are glazed over with lust as they connect with mine, and a sly smirk slowly forms on his lips.

He's so handsome I can't even stand it. Especially not in moments like this when he has his mouth on my clit, bringing me more pleasure than I've ever experienced.

I whimper when his tongue lashes at me, strumming along my clit. The pleasure is too much. Just when I feel like I'll burst open and see stars, he stops his assault.

"I have to talk to you about something."

His words vibrate against my center, and I groan in frustration. This is the worst form of torture.

I lace my fingers in his hair and pull him back toward where I want his mouth, and he grins. "I rented a cabin for next week. I have seven days off and we're going to Kettle Moraine, and I want you to come."

"Are we really having this conversation.... right now?" I screech. I'm laid out naked in front of him, with his head between my legs, and he wants to discuss next week's plans?

"We can discuss it in length, or you could just say yes." His warm breath fans along my inner thigh, causing goosebumps to erupt on my skin. I'm wound so tightly; I feel like I might pop at any moment. "And we could end it right here, I could give you exactly what you want..." He trails off then flicks his tongue against my clit once, then twice.

"Reed Davidson," I sit up on my elbows to stare down at him, "are you coercing me... by orgasm?"

"I'm offended, Holland, as if I ever would."

Yet the sheepish grin on his face says otherwise. His finger dips inside me, curling up and stroking until my back arches off the bed, my hands fist in the sheets, and his name tumbles from my lips.

So close, I can feel it.

Then he stops. Again.

"Reed!" I screech. "Stop it."

He laughs. "Say yes."

"No."

One finger becomes two and his lips close over my clit. He sucks and moves his fingers inside of me slowly, languidly, until I'm close again.

I arch closer to his mouth, desperate to finally fall over the edge he's teased me with, then he tears his mouth away and looks back up at me.

"Fine! God, fine."

"Really?"

"Yes, now will you please…" I trail off. A few seconds later, he's rising up and covering me with his hard, toned body and sliding inside of me in one smooth motion, filling me. It doesn't take long before we're both hot and sticky with sweat, Reed's fingers rubbing against my clit as we both come.

His muscular arms pull me onto his chest as he falls back against the bed. My ear's pressed against it, listening to his heart racing, and my eyes grow heavy.

"Are you really going to come?" he asks. I feel his lips against the top of my head.

I nod. "Not because you blackmailed me with an orgasm but because Emery already asked me and threatened bodily harm."

Reed scoffs. "So all of that and you already were going to come?"

"Yep. But you were so committed, I didn't want to stop you."

He laughs. "Such a sacrifice."

I lean back so I can look at him. "You know… I told her no. Several times, actually. I just- I'm worried that she'll know something is going on. She knows me better than anyone. I'm nervous."

Reed's quiet. He doesn't say anything about my fears, but his lips touch my hair again, and it brings me comfort.

"We're friends, babe. We always have been and Emery knows that. She's not going to suspect anything."

My nerves don't fade. I just hope that as well as Em knows me, she doesn't see right through me.

"I have to work late tonight," Emery says. "It's so lame, but we have this huge case that my boss is working on and we're all having to put in extra hours. I'm going to drive up later, so you'll have to ride up with Reed and Evan, but I won't be far behind you. You know my mom, she has to wake up at the crack of dawn and get there to make sure everything is ready."

My heart flips at the mention of Reed, but I laugh lightly. "Your mom is the most organized person I've ever met. I wish she would've rubbed off on either of us. I can ride with Reed and Evan, no problem. I was thinking I could maybe bring Dad, but I just don't know that he'll handle the change well. Mona said she was happy to stay with him."

I hate leaving him at home, but I know the importance of keeping him on schedule and in a place that is familiar for him. It's the one thing his doctor has been adamant about since he was diagnosed. I'm thankful that we have Mona, and she offered to stay with him extra this week in order for me to go with Em and her family.

"You need this, Holland. A few days away from responsibilities, studying, and work. It's going to be great," Emery says cheerily. "This is just what you need to relax and unwind."

My mind immediately drifts back to only a few days ago, when Reed was coaxing me into agreeing to this impromptu getaway with his mouth.

As happy as I am with Reed... Lately, my guilt seems to weigh heavier and heavier on both my heart and my mind.

This thing with Reed started as something uncomplicated, and now it feels like so much more. I should've known that I couldn't push my feelings aside and only have a physical relationship with him. Feelings complicate everything. Our situation is already complicated enough.

"Yeah, it's gonna be great. I can't wait to spend time with you. I'm gonna go start packing, and I'll see you later, okay? Drive safe."

"You too, babe. Love you, bye!"

We end the call, and I sit down next to my empty suitcase and stare at it.

You can do this, Holland. Three days cooped up with the guy you're secretly in love with, and your best friend who will probably murder you both if she finds out.

What better place than a secluded cabin in the middle of the woods, where no one will find our bodies?

I groan and flop back onto the bed.

It's *only* three days. I repeat the mantra for the rest of the afternoon as I pack, and before I know it, Reed's walking through my bedroom door, surprising me.

"All packed?" He trimmed his beard, and combed his wild curls back, making him look even more handsome. A red and black checkered print jacket is stretched over his broad shoulders paired with old, faded jeans and boots. "Evan's in the truck. We're ready when you are, babe." He drops a lingering kiss to my lips, and pulls back, holding my gaze.

Even though he's dressed for a camping trip, his attire isn't what stands out to me, it's the happiness in his eyes.

He's excited, and it shows in the smirk on his lips and the excitement behind his gaze. Don't get me wrong, I'm excited to get away and be with both Reed and Emery. But then... those two relationships can't go together, and it causes my stomach to lurch.

"You okay?" Reed asks, watching me put the last few things into my backpack.

I nod. "Just a little nervous about being in a cabin with Em... and I don't know. I'll be fine. I'm probably just overthinking it. I just hate lying to her, Reed."

His eyes soften. "I know. I was hoping we could talk when we get there tonight?"

"Okay."

He gives me another quick kiss before letting go to grab my suitcase off the bed. Dramatically, it falls to the floor heavily.

"Not this again." His eyes shine mischievously. "Better have that red lace in there that I love so much."

I roll my eyes. "Let's go, *Casanova*."

We get my suitcase loaded into the truck, and I slide into the passenger seat.

"Howwand!" Evan cries from the back seat. He's got Pickles tucked in close to his side, and his tablet in his lap. Reed was so torn on whether or not Evan should have a tablet at his age. He scoured the internet for hours, then ultimately decided to limit Evan's screen time and make sure the games he plays and the things he watches are educational.

It was the most "dad" thing ever, and it made my heart race a little faster. Seeing Reed change into this man I've never known has been so incredible. Watching him fall in love with Evan, and find himself as a parent is something you don't get to see every day. It makes me even more proud of him, and everything that the two of them have overcome together in the past months.

"Are you ready for a campfire and s'mores buddy?" I ask.

He shakes his head excitedly, his eyes lighting up the second I mention s'mores.

I continue, "It's my favorite thing about camping. S'mores!"

Reed opens the door and gets into the driver's seat.

"Are we ready?"

I nod, and Evan cheers.

It's go-time.

The ride to the cabin is surprisingly quiet, aside from Evan's babbling to Pickles. We ride in comfortable silence with Reed's hand resting on my thigh, and the other on the wheel. I focus on his touch, trying to soothe the nervous jitters in my stomach. Staring out the window, I watch the city fade behind us as we drive farther into the country, leaving the city limits behind.

We pull down a long, dirt road that's only gravel for what seems like forever before a small, adorably quaint cabin comes into view. It's the kind that you'd see in a Hallmark movie. Log on the outside, with a red front door and smoke billowing from the chimney. There's a stack of firewood piled against the side of the house, and a fire pit with large wooden chairs surrounding it that looks cozy, even without the fire going. I can see myself drinking a morning cup of coffee here.

It's perfect, so much so that I feel slightly less nervous. At least for now.

Reed parks in the driveway in front of the cabin, next to his mom's SUV, then comes around to open my door and get Evan out of his car seat.

The second my foot hits the soil and I inhale the fresh air, I smile. "Reed, this place is incredible."

"I'm glad you like it, babe. I figured everyone could use some time away, to refresh. The season's rough, and I wanted to take Evan and show him the outdoors." He smirks and looks at Evan who grins back cheekily.

"Holland Parker, is that you?" A soft, singsong voice comes from the porch. I turn around and see Reed and Emery's mom, Kathy, smiling warmly at me.

"You know it is. It's only been what, three weeks since I've seen you?" I smile and walk over into her open arms. She hugs me close to her body for a few moments before letting go.

Reed and Evan are on my heels, and she gives out extra hugs when it comes to Evan. He's obviously already got her wrapped around his little finger. Not that I can blame her... he's charming. Just like Reed.

"Now, Reed, grab those bags while we go inside and get warm." She visibly shivers and pulls her coat closed tighter. "These two are gonna freeze in this cold."

"Yes, Ma."

She grabs my hand after she scoops Evan up and drags me behind her into the cabin. I can't help but laugh. This is who Reed and Emery get their take-charge attitude from. One hundred percent their mom.

"Have you talked to Emery?" Kathy asks. "She said something about maybe having to work late."

"Yeah, she said she had to work late at the firm, but she'd be driving up afterward. That's why I rode with Reed and Evan. I don't feel comfortable driving when it snows heavily, so Reed offered to drive me."

She smiles. "That girl. Always working, but I guess I can admire her work ethic. You know she and Reed both have always been so driven by their goals. Reed would play outside with that hockey puck until it was so dark, they couldn't see it. You remember how he and his friends would put those cheap flashlights on the ice, just to get a few more minutes out there?"

I nod.

Boy, do I remember those days. Em and I were allowed to watch, since the pond was right behind their house, and we'd stand outside with our noses red and our lips chattering, just to watch them skate in the dark. The only light was from those damn flashlights that they'd beg us to hold. Even with gloves, my hands would be so cold, they'd go completely numb after only a few minutes, but I'd do it anyway since Reed was the one asking.

"I still get chills thinking about how cold I was then," I tell her.

It was the first time I realized that my crush had developed into something more, those nights with Reed on the ice. The sheer determination behind his shots. Despite the cold, the snow, his exhaustion, he pushed himself to the limits. He did whatever it took to reach the goal he set for himself.

The door opens, and Reed walks in carrying our bags, a bout of cold air coming with him. He disappears into the living room and comes back empty-handed.

"Evan, wanna go look for bears?" he asks. He's joking, but the look on Evan's face is priceless.

Evan's eyes widen, and he looks at me. I shrug. "That's up to you, Bud. I'm staying inside where it's warm and bear-free."

"I'm just kidding, but I did bring my stick from when I was younger. I'm gonna take Evan out to the pond. We'll be back before dark." He walks over to his mom and drops a sweet kiss on her cheek and tosses me a smile. Then he and Evan are walking outside, leaving Kathy and me alone in the kitchen.

"Mind helping me wash these potatoes for the stew?" she asks.

"Of course."

I take the bowl of potatoes from her and busy myself at the sink.

"You know, don't tell Emery I said this, but I think Reed is seeing someone," Kathy says from behind me.

I drop the bowl of potatoes and they land heavily in the sink with a loud clunk. Whipping around, I clear my throat nervously. "Why would you think that? It's Reed," I stammer.

She shrugs. "I know my boy. Perks of having boys, they're mama's boys. I know him like the back of my hand... it's just a feeling I get."

I swallow thickly, my throat suddenly feeling tighter than ever. Is it obvious? The way we act around each other? My nervous jitters morph into full-blown panic.

"I'm hoping he does settle down. He's not getting any younger, and if he could find someone that loves him and Evan... it's all I wish for my baby boy. To find love and happiness. In his profession, it's hard to determine who is genuine and not just out for the perks of being married to a hockey player. I think that's part of his problem, he has a hard time finding a genuine connection to anyone because of it." She looks up at me and smiles. "Sorry, I'm rambling, I just haven't ever seen him so happy. I can't help but wonder if it's something more than just Evan."

I nod shakily and drag my eyes back to the potatoes I'm mindlessly running water over. We finish prepping dinner in silence, but her words weigh heavy on my mind.

Why can't the way I feel about Reed be simple? Why does anyone have to be hurt because of how we feel about each other? Things aren't simple any longer; they're complicated, and I have a feeling if I'm not honest with myself, and Reed soon, I'll end up hurt.

CHAPTER EIGHTEEN

REED

The campfire crackles and pops. Its embers glowing orange and red in front of me. We're all sitting around the fire pit together while Evan and Ma make s'mores. I move my gaze from the fire to Holland, who's wrapped in a Sherpa jacket with a blanket draped over her shoulders, clutching a mug of hot chocolate and staring into the flames. I can see them lick and surge in the blue-glass reflection of her eyes.

"You okay?" I ask quietly. Ma's occupied with Evan, but I don't want to make Holland uncomfortable. She's been even more quiet than usual since I took Evan on the ice.

Holland nods. "Yeah." The smile on her lips doesn't reach her eyes, and I can tell that it's forced. I wish we were alone, so I could touch her. Hold her fucking hand and reassure her, but these rules we stupidly created prevent me from doing any of those things.

But tonight, it ends. I plan to tell her exactly how I feel.

"Evan, are you sleepy?" Ma asks him. I tear my gaze from Holland and glance at Evan. His eyes are heavy, and the stick he's holding with gooey marshmallow on it is starting to droop.

I laugh. "I think so. I can put him to bed." I start to rise from the chair, but Ma shakes her head and gives me a stern look. "You will not. I don't get enough time with him as it is. I'll get him ready for bed, and I'm going to turn in myself. I'm an old woman, I need my beauty rest."

"You're already beautiful, Ma," I tell her.

Her gaze softens. "You and Holland enjoy the fire for a bit. There's no sense in wasting a perfectly good fire. Plus, I think Emery will be here, at least I hope, before midnight. Wild girl."

Ma chides, but Emery is her only daughter, and she lets her get away with more stuff than I ever did.

"Come here, bud," I tell Evan. He pads over to me, and I scoop him up into my arms in a tight hug. "Goodnight, I'll see you in the morning, kay?"

He nods, rubbing his eyes sleepily.

Ma takes his hand and leads him inside. Now it's just Holland and me sitting in silence, with the sound of the sizzling fire.

"What's wrong, baby?" I ask. I know Holland. I've known her since she was the shy, nerdy little girl who was best friends with my sister and lived next door. And in the last six months, I've spent every bit of free time with her and Evan, getting to know the parts of her I only saw from a distance, and I know her. Like the back of my hand. Better than I've known anyone before.

She's been quieter, withdrawn, and she's keeping me at an arm's length. Completely unlike her, and I haven't wanted to press or make her feel like I was suffocating her. Especially because of these damn rules.

Holland looks up at me, tears shining in her deep blue eyes. "I can't do this anymore, Reed." Her words are merely a whisper, but they pack more of a punch than anything she's ever said.

It feels like a bucket of ice water has been dumped over my head. My fucking heart stops in my chest.

My voice is hoarse and raw as I croak, "What? What do you mean *this*? Our arrangement? Us?"

Our eyes are locked until she tears her tearful gaze away, and it feels like each second that passes, she's retreating further and further away from me. Maybe not physically, but right now, it feels like there's a fucking ocean separating us.

She lifts a shaky hand and covers her mouth as tears fall from her eyes.

Seeing her cry is like a knife to the heart. A white hot, brutal pain that I feel deep in my chest. I want to pull her into my arms, and say fuck the world, but it isn't that easy.

None of this is.

"I can't lie to Emery anymore. I can't keep secrets from my best friend. I can't *pretend* any longer." She looks away, staring off into the dark woods ahead of us then back to me, her gaze full of enough pain to hit me in the gut full force. "I can't pretend that this arrangement is working anymore. Those rules... they were never going to work. I should've known that before I agreed to this. I can't pretend that I don't have feelings for you any longer, Reed." Her lip quivers as she continues, "God, talking to your mom tonight… Reed, she thinks you're seeing someone. She said she's never seen you so happy. You deserve someone you can be with, out in the open, not in secret."

I stand from the chair and walk over to her, crouching down in front of her, sliding my hands up to cradle her jaw. She squeezes her eyes shut tightly, leaning in to my touch as steady tears fall down her cheeks.

"She's right. I've never been happy this way. Fuck, I've never felt like this *ever*. And it's terrifying. I've heard about this. From my teammates, my friends, from Liam. About how it feels to love someone."

She stills beneath my touch, but I don't stop. "That falling in love is the greatest feeling in the world, and they're not wrong. But it's also scary. That's the part that no one tells you about. The vulnerable, raw part of you that you're putting in another person's hands and praying that they love you for who you are. I love you, Holland. I am *in* love with you."

Hot tears fall from her blue eyes, and she lets out a small sob at my declaration. "I am not sorry for falling in love with you. I'm sorry that I had to do it in secret, when all I want to do is shout it from the rooftop of the tallest building in the whole damn city. I fucking love you, Holland. I thought I could never love anyone, that I was broken, that I was messed up from my father, but then you showed me otherwise. You and Evan are the only future I see. Those feelings you have? Baby, I feel them too and I have for a long time. I should've told you sooner, but I wasn't ready to be honest with myself, or with you. I had to figure it out the hard way."

"Reed," she cries. Her bottom lip trembles as she winds her hands through my hair to the back of my neck. This moment, it's everything I've been holding inside, and fuck, it feels good to say it out loud. To tell her how I feel, even if I'm petrified of fucking it up. Of letting myself get hurt. Of hurting her.

I press my forehead to hers. "I can't go back, Holland. I can't go back to the way things were before. Not when I know what it's like to love you."

She nods against me. "I... I love you too, Reed."

It's heaven hearing her say it.

A heaven I never thought I'd be worthy enough to enter.

Without another thought, I capture her lips with mine, kissing her with every ounce of love that I've been holding inside for months. I want everyone to know. This is *my* girl. Mine. She pulls on my hair as I kiss her breathless, and my tongue tangles with hers. I wrench my lips from hers to stare into her stormy eyes.

"I made new rules for us. In my head, I've been going over them every time I thought about how to tell you this. To tell you that I fell in love with you despite those damn rules. I've come to hate them, so I made new ones."

I sit back and hold her eyes as a small grin tugs at the corner of my lips. "One: Fall in love every day. Never stop showing you how much you mean to me, and giving you reasons to fall in love with me."

She covers her mouth and she squeezes her eyes shut as

her mascara runs down her face. God, even now, she's fucking beautiful.

"Two: Shout it to the world. I'm never going to not show my love for you. I want everyone in the goddamn world to know that I'm the bastard that's lucky enough to love you, Holland Parker. I'll put it on the jumbotron. On every damn billboard in Chicago."

"And three: Always stay stocked with gummy worms." Holland tosses her head back and lets out a watery laugh. It makes me chuckle. "I mean it, babe. I promise to always have them on hand, because I can't imagine not having you with me and Evan. At night, in the morning, every fucking day. You're the only one for me, Holland."

"I don't know how to tell Emery this. How do I tell her that I lied to her and fell in love with her brother? I'm scared to lose her. She's my best friend, Reed."

"We take it day by day. We sit down, think of what we're going to say, and then we do it. She's going to be angry, I'm sure. She's like a feisty little Pomeranian, she'll probably try and bite my fucking head off. But my sister has a heart of gold, and you know that. She'll eventually forgive us."

Holland bites her lip, and I can still see the hesitation in her eyes. The fire has started to die, and I can feel her starting to shiver.

"Babe, we have to go inside, you're fucking freezing."

"I am pretty cold," she says quietly, "I just need to time to process this. It's a lot and I just... I need some time, okay?"

"I'm not going anywhere. Take as much time as you need. I just needed you to know how I felt, and that what I feel for you, it's not going away."

I stand and take her hand and wait for her to gather the blanket she had around her shoulders before we make our way into the cabin. It's dark and quiet inside, and I know Ma's already asleep.

"My room's at the end of the hallway, and yours is right here."

Even though it's only three doors down, it feels like she's across the damn world right now. But I'll respect her wishes for space. I put the ball in her court tonight, and I understand her need to sort through everything. Hell, I've spent the past few months trying to figure out my own shit.

"Goodnight, Reed." She lifts up on her tiptoes and kisses me, quick and sweet, then opens the door and closes it shut quietly behind her.

I stare at the door once she's gone, hoping that the conclusion she comes to is that she wants this just as much as I do. My chest feels lighter, and I'd be lying if I said I wasn't glad that I confessed my feelings to her, to have it off my chest and in the open. I walk to the room Evan's in and peek inside to make sure he's okay. His sea-animal light is spinning blue and green shapes onto the ceiling, and he's fast asleep, still clutching Pickles. Shutting the door, I head to my room and walk inside.

It's going to be a long fucking night, knowing Holland is right down the hall, and I can't touch her. After a shower and spending hours tossing and turning, I fall asleep. The last time I looked at the glowing numbers on the clock, it was two thirty. The sound of my door creaking open and the covers being pulled back causes me to stir.

I crack open one eye and see Holland sliding into bed next to me. I wrap the covers back around us, to keep in the warmth, and loop my arm around her, pulling her against me.

"I couldn't sleep. I needed to see you," she murmurs, peppering kisses along my jaw. Her cold hands slip under the hoodie I tossed on, to rest on my stomach, and I grin. My girl and her cold hands and feet. She's constantly putting them on me to steal some of my body heat.

I'm still half asleep, but fuck, I'm glad she's here.

"I really want some Captain Crunch, but it didn't feel right to sneak any without you."

I laugh. "Is that so? I'm glad you didn't, because then I'd have to label you a traitor."

She sits up and smirks. "Better come on then." The covers are tossed back and she's tiptoeing down the hallway before I can even get out of the bed. I climb out and follow behind her into the kitchen. She's on her tiptoes, trying to get the box from on top of the fridge, and I come up behind her, pressing her against it. Her sweet, pert ass brushes along my length, and in any other circumstance, I'd fuck her right here, having her clutch the fridge for dear life, but alas… I have to behave.

She giggles when I reach past her head and get the box. "I can't help it you're a giant."

Leaning down, I whisper into her ear, "Babe, it doesn't help my ego when you talk about how big I am."

Her elbow connects lightly with my stomach, and I laugh, handing her the box, but before she can grab a bowl, I pull her back against me and kiss the sensitive spot behind her ear, trailing down to the column of her neck.

"Might wanna set that box down, Holl."

She puts it on the counter and holds on to the edge with white knuckles as my hands roam her tight body. God, these curves. I'm fucking crazy about her and them. I slide my hands down her hips to the front of her stomach and dip under the waistband of her sleep shorts, past the scrap of lace covering her sweet pussy, then drag my fingers through her slit. When my fingers connect, she hisses.

"Mmm," Holland moans quietly, and I tease her clit faster as I feel the tension in her body build.

"Reed? Holland?" Emery's voice breaks through the darkness. Holland jumps so fast, she knocks into me, and I straighten her shorts to make sure she's covered.

Shit. Shit. SHIT.

Not only did Emery just catch us at the worst possible time, she caught us with my hand down Holland's shorts.

The light flicks on and Emery's standing in front of us, a mask of shock on her face. She's still got on her jeans and coat with fresh snow on her shoulders, so she must have just gotten to the cabin. We were so caught up in the moment that we didn't even hear the front door open.

"What the hell?" she screeches.

Holland visibly shrinks back and tries to walk toward her. "Emery, I..."

Em holds her hand up, stopping her. "Wow. So this is why you've been so checked out? This is what you've been hiding from me?" Her eyes dart back and forth between Holland and me.

Take the worst possible scenario and multiply it times three and this is the disaster that is happening right the fuck now. This is the absolute worst way for Emery to find out.

"Please, just listen Eme-" Holland starts, but Emery cuts her off. Tears shine in Emery's eyes as she looks at her.

"God, Holland, you've been my best friend my entire life. And you lied to me? Hid this from me? To what... sleep with my *brother*?" Emery sneers. "I can't believe you'd do this. Either of you. Especially not you, Holland."

I can feel the anger vibrate off of her. When I step toward her, she takes a step back.

"Just let us explain, Em," I try, and she shakes her head vehemently, mascara-streaked tears wetting her cheeks.

"I don't want to speak to either of you. *You* can explain to Mom why I left; I can't be here right now. I'm out."

She turns and wrenches the door open, storming out and letting it slam shut behind her. So hard that the door vibrates in the frame.

God, this is a fucking nightmare.

I look over at Holland, who's already starting to cry. Her small shoulders shaking.

"Baby." I reach for her, and she pulls away and brushes past me toward her room. I hear the door shut, and the lock click.

I walk over to the door and knock lightly, not being able to stand the fact that she's hurting and this fucking door is separating us, but she doesn't answer.

Looking over at the front door, I decide to go after Emery. I grab my jacket from the coatrack and slip my boots on. I open the door and walk outside to search for Emery. I get it, she's pissed off and wants nothing to do with us right now, but it's not safe for her to be out here in the middle of the damn night.

My eyes scan the driveway in the dark, and realize her car is gone. She left.

I walk back inside in search of my phone; I grab it off the charger then call her. It rings, then goes to voicemail, so I try once... twice... three more times.

Damnit, Emery. Pick up the phone.

This time it goes straight to voicemail. I type out a text to her.

Me: I know you're pissed, Em, but please be safe. It's dark and the roads are slick.

A few seconds later, the read receipt pops up, so at least I know she saw the message. The response bubbles start and a text from her comes through.

Emery: I'm not answering the phone, so stop calling. You're an asshole and I don't want to talk to you, Reed. But I'm not stupid. I'll be fine. I need space. Please give me space.

I fucking hate this. I hate fighting with Em. I can count on one hand the number of actual arguments or real disagreements we had growing up, so one like this hits me square in the chest. I just wish that she would've given us a moment to explain, so she could see that the feelings I have for Holland are genuine before she blew up and stormed out.

If there's one thing Emery is, it's passionate. I'll respect her wishes for space for now, but I can't let her stay angry at me. Not over this.

Sighing, I shove my phone in the pocket of my hoodie and walk back to Holland's door. I want to knock again and check on her, to make sure she's okay, but I also don't want her to pull away from me anymore than she did the past few days.

Hopefully by morning, she'll want to talk, and we can figure all of this out together. Because, even though Emery is angry at us right now, and I knew that it would inevitably happen, my feelings for Holland aren't going to change. The sooner I can explain that to Emery, the better.

I walk back to my room, shed my clothes and climb into bed and under the covers. The last thing I remember thinking before I fall asleep is that the sheets still smell like Holland, and how even though tonight didn't go at all how I planned, I don't regret it for a fucking second.

CHAPTER NINETEEN

REED

I've had a lot of injuries in my career. Broken bones, concussions, gashes from being thrown against the boards by two-hundred-and fifty-pound powerhouses. I'm no stranger to pain.

But the five days I've spent without Holland are by far the most painful ones of my entire fucking life. I'm a mess. So much so that Liam's currently sitting across from me, looking at me like I've lost my mind.

Probably have.

Holland hasn't spoken to me in five days. My fucking sister hasn't spoken to me in five days. Both of them have ignored my calls, my texts, the flowers that I had sent.

Dead silence.

And I miss her. God, I miss her laugh, I miss those fucking gummy worms. I miss her making fun of me every chance she gets.

I'm in a grumpy ass mood and now Liam is trying his version of an intervention. I don't need an intervention; I need my girl. I need this mess to be over, and my sister not to be angry and my entire world not to be flipped on its ass.

"You're not sitting here another day moping. Fuck, Reed, I've never seen you play so shitty in your life." Liam grunts, kicking my Nike covered foot off of the ottoman onto the floor with more force than necessary.

"I'm not moping, shut up."

He looks at me incredulously. "Listen to yourself. Get up. Go shower and pull your head out of your ass. Go to Emery, talk to her. Tell her what you're feeling and end this shit."

"It's not that simple, Liam, she won't even respond to my texts."

"Then go over there. Your mom isn't going to slam the door in your face. Sitting across the damn city from each other, being pissed off, isn't going to solve anything. Take a shower first, you smell like sweaty socks."

"You're a dick," I tell him begrudgingly, getting up from the couch and sniffing my armpit to check.

Damnit, I smell like *ass*.

"Shut up," I bark when he smirks.

"It's what I'm here for. I'm going to take Evan to the park with the girls and then to a movie, call me later."

I walk by Evan's room and he's currently taking his ships and wrecking them into the tall Lego castle he's built and rebuilt five times.

"Hey, bud, wanna go to the park with Uncle Liam, Ari and Ken?"

He drops the ship like it's on fire and squeals, "Yes, please!" I make sure his backpack is packed, and he grabs Pickles from his bed, and I hand it over to Liam.

"He's got extra pull-ups in there. We're working on the potty, but sometimes, he still has accidents, so make sure you tell him when to go because he gets busy playing and he forgets and-"

"Dude. I have two kids, and a baby on the way," Liam says.

Shit.

"Sorry, habit."

Liam claps me on the back. "Told you that you'd be an awesome Dad. Don't worry about Evan. He'll be having a blast. Worry about fixing the mess that you made."

Easier said than done. I grumble to myself and shut the door behind them. Even though I know I need to, I am dreading seeing Emery. She's liable to run me over with her car. She's that mad. In our entire lives, we've never gone more than a weekend without speaking and now five days have passed.

After a quick shower, and change of clothes, I grab my keys and phone and head to my truck. I think about what I'm going to say the entire drive.

More like rehearse my apology and hope that Emery isn't feeling like doing bodily harm.

There's only one person in this world who scares me, and she's five-foot-one and thinks coffee is a major food group.

Seriously, she's fucking scary. Like a little rabid dog when she's angry.

When I pull my truck into Ma's driveway and put it in park, I let out a deep breath and step out.

I can fucking do this. I walk up the drive and to the front door then knock, before opening it.

"Ma? Emery?" I call. I kick my shoes off at the door, because that's all I need, two angry Davidson women. Ma will beat my ass if I track dirt in her house.

I walk around the corner into the living room and see Emery perched on the couch, looking as rough as I fucking feel.

Her hair is in a knot on the top of her head, with strands flying in twenty different directions. Her mascara is smeared down her cheeks. The rims of her eyes are red and puffy, like she's been crying. She's in her pajamas on the couch with candy boxes surrounding her.

"What are you doing here?" she mutters, not taking her gaze off the tv. I glance at the big screen and realize she's watching *One Tree Hill.*

Jesus, I really fucked up. *One Tree Hill* is Emery's comfort show. If that shit's on, then something irreparably bad has happened. How do I know this? Oh, you know, growing up in a house with two women, I've been subjected to more torture than you can imagine over the years. I should've brought Starbucks.

"Em." I speak her name quietly.

Her red-rimmed eyes flick to mine before she rolls them. "Fine. Sit."

I walk over and flop down next to her, stealing the box of

gummy worms out of her hands. She cuts her eyes at me then sighs.

The candy reminds me of Holland and causes an ache in my chest. Fuck, I miss her.

"You look like shit," Emery says too cheerily.

"Feel like shit too." I grunt.

We sit in silence, both of us staring at the tv.

"You know, you could've just told me." She looks over at me. "About you and Holland."

"Em, you would've murdered me in my sleep. Literally."

Emery shrugs, popping another gummy worm in her mouth. "I *should* murder you in your sleep now, for lying to me and hiding shit from me. She's my best friend, Reed. And I fucking know you. You have a track record for breaking hearts, and Holland is too good. She's too pure to be tainted by your manwhore ways."

Her words hurt, a little. But only because they're fucking true. Before Holland, and before Evan... I was different. I drank too much, partied even more, and spent more nights with women whose names I can't even remember to this day. I always respected them by being upfront about what they would get when they were with me, but it was nothing more than a one-night kind of thing.

I've never been in a relationship, never been in love. That's how I know what I feel for Holland is real, and fuck is it genuine. There's nothing in the world I wouldn't do for her.

"I love her, Em," I say quietly. It feels unreal to say the words out loud to Emery, but fuck, it's a weight off my chest. Because even if Holland decides to never pick up the phone for me again,

I'll always love her.

She sits up straight and looks at me with wide eyes. "You love Holland?"

I nod. "Fuck, I'm scared. I'm scared I'll fuck this up and do something that hurts her. I'd rather jump in front of a moving truck than ever hurt her. Not like being with another woman because she's it for me. But, not giving her everything that I can. What if I end up like Dad?"

Em takes my hand. "Reed Davidson, don't ever say that again. I am pissed off at you more than I've ever been in my life and I can still say that you are twice the man that he will ever be. You have been the best big brother my entire life. Picked up all of the pieces he left behind. You are nothing like him."

"She taught me how to love, Em. It's not like we conspired behind your back to hurt you. You know how much that girl loves you? She would give me up in a heartbeat if it meant keeping you. She left. The next morning when I woke up, she was gone. Uber'ed back to the city. Left a note and said she needed space, to please not contact her. I feel like I'm fucking dying."

I sit up and drop my head into my hands, running my hand through the mop on my head.

"Holy shit, you really do love her," Emery murmurs in a shocked, hushed tone. "I never thought I'd see the day that someone knocked you on your ass and it just so happens to be my best friend. I'm mad, but damn, I'm kinda proud." She turns toward me and pulls her knees up to her chest before speaking again. "Reed, I don't care if you're in love with Holland. I mean, I'm happy for you guys. I just… it hurt me so bad that you both lied to me, and hid this from me. Why wouldn't you just tell me?"

Fuck, when she says it like that I feel like a total asshole. Even more so now.

"Em, Holland was terrified that you would hate her, and I didn't want to hurt you, especially for something that started as a temporary arrangement." When she winces and scrunches her nose, I laugh. "Sorry. At first it was supposed to be casual, just hooking up, and then… it wasn't. I fell in love with her, even though it was against the rules."

"Rules?"

"We made a list of rules that were supposed to keep things simple, and it did anything but keep shit simple. If anything, it complicated everything. I'm sorry for keeping it from you, Em. I know Holland is too. It was important to Holland that you didn't get hurt because of it, and I'm sorry that it blew up in our faces, and you had to find out this way. But I'm not sorry for loving her. We planned that night that we were going to tell you, and then it all went to shit before we could."

Emery groans. "God, you really do love her. It's okay, you big douche. But you better promise to never lie to me again, or I will have to hurt you."

I nod. "I swear."

"And if you hurt her, well then, I'm going to hurt you. So beware."

"Yeah, well, she won't even talk to me, so I don't think you have to worry about that."

Emery flops back onto the couch dramatically, sighing. "I should talk to her. I need to talk to her. I'm not even mad at her for banging my brother. I'm just angry that she's my best friend and she lied to me."

"I know."

We sit together silently before Em springs up. "You know what. I'm going there."

I raise my eyebrows. "Right now?"

"Yeah, sure, why not, she lives next door, you dork. I'll see you later, okay?"

Is she kicking me out right now?

"Are you seriously kicking me out of Mom's?"

She nods. "Go. I have things to fix, and people to see. Goodbye." Her singsong voice carries into the other room.

Just like that, she's gone, disappearing into her room, and I'm left sinking into the couch, wishing it was that easy to get Holland to speak to me.

CHAPTER TWENTY
HOLLAND

"I got it," I call out to Dad when the doorbell rings. Grumbling, I make my way to the front door and swing it open, revealing Emery on the other side.

I'm so shocked I stutter, "E-m?"

She rolls her eyes and pushes past me into the house then grabs my hand and drags me behind her, so quickly I can hardly shut the door behind her. "This fight is officially over."

And just like that, my best friend is back, doing what she does best.

"Sit," she commands when we get into my room. Knowing how upset she is with me, I sit without another word.

"You have to go to Reed."

Of all the things I expected her to say, this was *not* it.

"Wait, what?"

Emery huffs. "Holland, you are my best friend, and for someone so incredibly intelligent, you sure can be stupid sometimes." She grins.

"You're not... mad at me?"

Shrugging, she sits cross-legged next to me on my bed. "I mean, am I hurt? Hell yeah. We've been best friends since we were kids, Holl, and you lied to me. You purposely hid things from me with my brother." She shudders and gags dramatically. "That hurts. I was never mad at you because you and Reed are together. I was shocked, duh. But it was more about the fact that you didn't think enough of me to tell me."

"Em, that's not it at all. I just... I was so afraid to lose you. I was scared that you'd hate me and I couldn't lose you. I remember when we first became friends, how much you hated all of the girls who used you just to be with Reed. That hurt you, Em. I never wanted to be that person, you're my best friend. Our friendship is everything to me."

Emery shakes her head. "Holland, I would never think that about you. I mean, yeah, those girls fucking sucked, but it was also forever ago, and since then I bossed up, grew thicker skin, and became a badass bitch. I wish we could've talked about it so all of this could have been avoided, babe. I'm not angry you and Reed are... a thing."

I exhale slowly, in relief. The weight I had been carrying around for months is suddenly lifted and I can finally take a deep breath.

"I think you should go talk to Reed, though. He's a mess, Holland. You need to talk to him."

I exhale. "God, I screwed this all up. I pushed him away."

She pulls me against her chest and wraps her arms around me, hugging me tightly to her.

"Smart people can be stupid sometimes, but you acted with your heart. You have the best heart of anyone I know, Holland."

"Well, since we're being honest, I need to tell you something else." I sit up and take a deep breath. "I've had feelings for Reed... for a really long time. Like, since we were kids."

Emery's jaw drops. She sputters, "You have?"

I nod. "I didn't want our friendship to end because of how I felt. And I just didn't ever think I'd even be on Reed's radar. He doesn't even know how I feel. I've never told anyone, until you right now."

"You have to tell him! God, Holl, this is like one of those freaking romance novels you're constantly reading."

It feels like it. I miss Reed, and I've hated every second of the past week. Being apart from him was torture, but I thought I was doing the right thing. I didn't want to be the reason that his relationship with Emery was strained, and Em and I weren't even speaking.

"I told him I needed space. I didn't know what to do, Em..." I trail off.

"Look, the thing with relationships is they aren't perfect. Nothing about them. You're both going to fuck up, you're both going to make mistakes. But what does matter? It's that you communicate and learn to work together through problems."

"You know for a perpetually single girl, you sure do have the best relationship advice."

Emery shrugs. "It's a gift."

"I promise. I never want to have an argument again. It was torture, Em. I wanted to give you space, but I picked up the phone so many times to call you and I didn't think you'd answer, so I've just been sitting here, wallowing in my sorrows."

Em lies back on my bed, staring at the stars on the ceiling, and I lie down next to her.

"Me too. I was watching reruns of *One Tree Hill* and hating Peyton all over again. Do you remember when you put these up? How we'd stare at them for hours and talk about boys, and listen to One Republic like it was going out of style."

I laugh. "Oh God. Yes. Those were the days. I had those bangs, do you remember how hideous they were? Never let me get bangs again, please."

"I loved your bangs, but okay, fine." Em looks at me. "I missed you, Holl."

"Missed you, Em. I'm sorry about all of this. If I could do it over, I would do things differently. A lot of things, really."

"Just remember, babe, hoes before bros. I love you and I'm always here."

I give her another tight hug before I pull back and look at her. "I think I have an idea… when I go talk to Reed. Do you think you can help me?"

She sits up. "Do you even have to ask? Hit me, bitch."

So I tell her my plan, and pray that it's not too late.

The glass box in my hands shakes as I struggle to switch it from one hand to the other in order to ring the doorbell. Seeing as how it's almost as big as me and I'm struggling to hold it, period.

I am failing. Damnit. I'm going to drop this thing.

Just as I'm bending to set it down on the porch, the front door swings open and when I look up, Reed and Evan are standing in the doorway staring at me.

A whoosh of breath leaves my lungs, seeing Reed for the first time since the cabin. It never lessens the racing of my heart whenever I see him. Every time is like the first time. I'm, somehow, taken aback by how handsome he is.

He's gotten his hair cut since I've seen him and it's shorter, more tamed, and I wish that I could reach out and run my hands through it, making the curls I love so much unruly again.

"Holland?" Reed asks, his brow furrowed.

He's confused that I'm here, and he has every right to be. I pushed him away, and asked for space, and now here I am on his doorstep, clutching an aquarium that's bigger than I am.

"Hi," I say quietly, "umm, I don't really know where to start, but this is really heavy, can I bring it inside?"

He hurriedly steps outside and takes it from my hands before turning back and walking through the front door. I follow behind him, suddenly even more nervous than I was when I rehearsed this conversation fifty times in my head.

My palms are clammy, my heart is racing in my chest.

Evan slides his hand in my sweaty palm and grins up at me. "Is dat for me, Howwand?"

I nod. "Yeah, buddy, this is for you."

Letting his hand go, I pull out a bag from inside the waterless aquarium.

"I guess I should start by saying I'm sorry. I shouldn't have pushed you away."

"Holland, you don't have to apologize," Reed says.

"No, I do. You poured your heart out to me, which took courage, and I ran when I thought I had lost Emery. I was scared, Reed. Not just about hurting Emery or the fact that she found out about us the way that she did. I was scared that I would end up hurt."

Still clutching the bag, I step closer. "I have a confession too. When we agreed to the rules, to this arrangement, or whatever you want to call it... I was holding a secret then. Reed, I've been in love with you since I was a kid. Since I was the dorky, shy, little sister's best friend who didn't even register on your radar."

"What?" Reed says hoarsely.

I nod. "I'm sorry that it took me so long to tell you that. I'm sorry that I didn't have the courage to admit to you how I really felt. And I'm sorry that those feelings, and the blow up with Emery, caused me to push you away, when I really should have pulled you closer."

Reed steps toward me, and if my hand wasn't full, I would

reach out to touch him, but alas, I'm not to this part of the apology yet. "I love you. And I'm sorry that it took me so long to say that too. I've loved you since the first time you beat up Marcus in the eighth grade because someone called me a cow. Since the time I sprained my ankle and you carried me all the way home from the ice that day. From the very day we made the rules and said not to fall in love. It was too late then. I was already crazy about you."

I hold up the sea creature inside the plastic bag, and Evan's eyes widen when he sees it swimming about.

"So, here I am, being completely and totally honest with you. Asking that you give me another chance because love is scary, and love is hard sometimes, but it doesn't mean that it's not worth it. And I bought this dwarf seahorse because I went to the pet store and they looked at me like I was insane when I asked for a live octopus, and apparently, they don't carry them because they're actually really aggressive animals and are really quite large and..."

Before I can even finish rambling, the sea horse is taken out of my hand and Reed's yanking me to him and his lips are on mine. I missed him so much my chest ached and I didn't realize how much until now.

When he pulls his mouth from mine and gazes at me, with a smirk on his lips, for the first time in a week, I feel like everything is going to be okay.

"Baby, I can't believe that we just spent the past week apart over something so damn stupid."

I nod, scrunching my nose. The entire thing could have been

avoided had we just been honest with Emery… and ourselves.

"That's what a relationship is. It's learning to communicate and fix problems when things go awry. I'm learning. We're learning. I promise no matter what, I won't push you away. I'll voice how I feel, and together, we can handle it."

Reed leans down and kisses me again, so much that I'm breathless and my train of thought is completely disarrayed.

I pull back and nod toward the bag on the table. "This is Dill. Dill the dwarf seahorse. You know because octopuses are poisonous and kind of," I lean in and whisper, "assholes. But he can be Pickles's friend."

Reed shakes his head. "I fucking love you." He looks down at Evan who's got his nose pressed against the aquarium. "Evan, buddy, Holland got an actual sea creature just for you."

Evan nods. His little nose has made smear marks on the glass and it makes me laugh.

"Let's get him set up in his new home. Where should we put him?" Reed asks.

Don't say his room.

"My room!" Evan says and runs off in the direction of his bedroom.

Once he's out of earshot, I look at Reed. "No way. He'll end up with his hand in the tank before the night is over. Trust me. How about in the living room, on the sofa table?"

"Good idea."

I help Reed set up the aquarium, and before I know it, the sun has gone down and Evan's yawning.

"Are you tired, buddy?" I ask.

He shakes his head sleepily. I've missed him just as much as I've missed Reed.

I spend the next hour with Evan. Bathing him, helping him pick out his pajamas, spending more time gazing at Dill before his eyes are so heavy, he's nodding off sitting up.

Motioning to Reed, I get him to grab Pickles from the counter and I carry Evan into his room, tucking him into bed. Reed sets Pickles down next to him, turns on his nightlight and then we walk out together.

"You know, it's almost like we're a... team." Reed grins before he squats down and throws me over his shoulder.

I yelp loudly. "Oh god, Reed Aaron, put me down! Right now!"

When he smacks my ass, not once, but twice, I squeal. He's carrying me to his room, and once we're inside, he tosses me down onto the bed.

"I haven't gotten a solid night's sleep since the cabin. Time to pay up."

He grins then climbs over me. His hard body molding to mine.

I haven't slept either. If anything, I've spent more time wishing I was with him.

"Me either. I'm glad I got to talk to Em. Without her...You know, it's kind of funny, she was the reason we decided to keep things a secret in the first place. And she ended up being the one that pushed us back together. It's important to me to have her blessing."

His dark, chocolate eyes hold mine and he nods. "She's Em. Nothing would be the same if not for her dramatic productions. Love her, but it's the truth. You know I've been thinking a lot over the past five days."

"About?" I ask.

"You. Us. Evan," Reed pulls me into his body, dropping kisses along my jaw, "I think you should move in with us.

I'm so shocked that I sit up abruptly and in the process bump into Reed.

"Shit," he curses, clutching his nose.

"I'm sorry, I'm so sorry. You can't just spring that on me, Reed, my *god*."

His eyes are squeezed tightly shut, but he shrugs. "Felt like as good of a time as any. We said we wanted to communicate and be honest with each other, and I want you to move in with me. Hell, I've lived next door to you practically our entire lives. If there is anything I've learned in the past week, it's to say what you feel and do it from the start. Don't beat around the bush and pretend that it's anything different. I want you here, Holland. I want you in my bed, in my truck, in the stadium when I take home the fucking Stanley Cup. I love you and I want our life to be together. With me. With Evan. With Pickles. And Dill. To be a family. *My* family."

God, this man. He's always making me cry with his words. He's thoughtful and kind, and it's hard to believe that he's mine sometimes, and now... the entire world can know. After this, I never want to keep another secret when it comes to Reed.

I lean toward him, more carefully this time, and kiss him. His hands cradle my jaw and his thumb absentmindedly rubs my cheek.

"I love you too. And Evan. And Pickles. And Dill. And I want that too, more than anything. I want to wake up every day with you, and make you watch all the scary movies that you hate, and stock your house with gummy worms. I also have to think of my dad. It's just been him and me for a really long time. I've always taken care of him, and I can't leave him there alone."

Reed nods. "I know, baby. What if we move him in too? There's plenty of room for him in this house and nothing would make me happier than having you both here."

"I've been thinking a lot about Serenity Ranch. I want to bring him and see what he thinks about it, see if it would be something good for him. It's incredible, and it's an option for his future that we never had before. Thanks to you. I would've never known about it, Reed."

He leans down to kiss me, slow and sweet. "You don't have to make a decision now, baby, but whenever you're ready, I'll be here. I support whatever you decide. You know, another thing I've been thinking about lately? Our love is a lot like my favorite hockey term."

"And what's that?"

"Change on the fly. You don't stop, you change what you have to and finish out the game."

It does relate a lot to Reed and me, and the changes we've gone through. What started as a childhood crush became so much more. And even with the bumps in the road, it was the best decision I ever made. That's the thing about love. It's messy. It's not always easy. It's not always perfect. It has to be willing to change, to reshape, to grow.

To become more than you ever thought possible.

And I found that in Reed Davidson, when I least expected it, and I am *never* letting it go.

EPILOGUE

REED
ONE YEAR LATER

"Alright buddy, you ready?"

Evan nods. "I'm weady, weed!"

It's been a full year since the day I brought Holland to Serenity Ranch for the very first time, and to say our lives have changed feels like an understatement. The good thing is, change is kind of our thing. We take it as it comes, and we adapt.

Evan turned four a few months ago, and Holland and I made the decision to put him in preschool here in Chicago. That meant they were no longer on the road with me, and damn I miss them but, ultimately, I know it's what is best for Evan. The Avalanche went on to win the Stanley Cup for the second year in a row, and to say that seems pretty *unfuckingreal*, but we did and I'm proud as hell of my team for doing it.

Today, we're headed back to Serenity Ranch to visit Holland's dad, Mike. Six months ago, when Holland decided to move in with me, it was only after Mike had really started to thrive with the staff and people at Serenity. He'd been going there for six months and it was obvious it was improving, not just his condition, but his happiness as well.

He still has bad days. There's no cure for Alzheimer's, but those bad days are far outweighed by the good ones. Just last month, we spent the entire day in his workshop, tinkering with his boat. Even though it hasn't been run in over five years, he remembers it like it was only yesterday and that's what I continue to let him believe.

That day changed my life too.

"Hey Mike, I have a question for you."

"Hmm?" Mike looks up at me, oil smeared on his face and a wrench between his lips. From the outside looking in, you'd never know he has a disease that steals his mind every day. Not on a day like today where it feels like all of those years ago, when Holland was just the girl next door, and I was just her best friend's brother.

"I'm asking for your permission to propose to Holland. I want to marry her, sir."

His eyes fill with unshed tears, and he nods. "You have my blessing, Reed. Always knew you two would end up together."

"You did?" I ask.

Mike nods then shrugs. "Just the matter of you both figurin' it out. Bout dang time."

His smile makes my heart constrict, and I hold out my hand for him to shake. He bypasses it and pulls me into a hug. "Gonna give you a piece of advice, son. One that I don't want you to ever forget. Love each other, even when it's hard. Never go to bed mad, and always put your family first."

"I will, Mike, I promise you."

"Welcome to the family, son, now are you going to help me with this motor or stand there like a pretty boy?"

I grin and take the wrench from his extended hand.

I'll never forget that moment. Even twenty years from now, I'll remember Mike and the advice he gave me in that workshop.

Today, I'm making good on that promise and I'm proposing to Holland.

It's just Evan and me, standing near the horse stable, waiting for her to walk around the corner. I'm not nervous for what I'm about to do.

I know without a doubt that Holland is our future. There's never been any question. Not since that first night she sat next to me, shoving gummy worms into her mouth without a care in the world.

She's been my girl, through it all.

Evan slides his clammy little hand into mine, and I grasp it tightly. He doesn't really know what's happening today, but he knows that it's important, and hopefully, one day, he looks back and knows how important he is to me. How much he changed my life.

Without Evan, I wouldn't be the man I am today. I've done a lot of changing over the past year. I've learned patience, understanding, and how to be a father. How to learn from my mistakes and not make the same ones over and over. How to love this little boy who has put his trust in me to take care of him. I've learned how to half-ass paint pictures, how to build Lego castles and to always check pockets before I do the laundry. Well, that one is more for Holland than me, and the thought makes me grin.

I've cleaned cuts and scrapes, checked under the bed for invisible monsters, and held my little guy when a bad dream left him in tears.

It hasn't always been easy, but it's been worth it. Over and over again.

Suddenly, I see a flash of Holland's blonde hair, and she comes around the corner with a wide smile. Her eyes meet mine, and she looks between Evan and me and her brow furrows.

"Reed? Evan? I thought you were at the cabin?"

That's what I had my Ma and Em tell her, but I planned to be here the entire time, that box in Evan's pocket.

"Had something else more important to take care of."

She finally walks up and stands in front of us, her cheeks red from chasing around Polly, the goat that has stolen her heart. She has straw in her hair, dirt on her chin, but happiness in her eyes.

This place changed all of us.

Now seems like as good a time as any, so right there in the dirt on the ranch, I drop to one knee. Holland's eyes go wide, and she covers her mouth.

"When I think about my future, about our future, you're all I see. There's no scenario in my life where you're not in it. I thought I knew who I was before I met you. I thought I had it all mapped out. I thought I knew exactly how it was gonna go and then you changed everything. I think I loved you the second your classic novel almost impaled me on the floor of your basement. Maybe even before then."

I take her trembling hand in mine before continuing, "Marry me. Next year, next week, tomorrow. I don't care. Just marry me. Be my wife. I want to spend the rest of my life waking up to you, reminding you that you are the only woman I will ever love. You've taught me how to be a better man. To be patient, to put my socks in the hamper and put the toilet seat down. You've taught me how to love. I need you now and for the rest of my life. I promise to love you through whatever trials we face, and hold your hand when things get hard. To never go to bed upset and to always put our family first."

Looking over at Evan, he steps forward, a shy expression on his face as he pulls the box from his pocket. "Howwand, will you maww-ee Weed and stay with us *forever*?"

Oh fuck, he did it even better than we practiced.

Holland sobs and shakes her head profusely. "Of course I will." She drops to her knees in front of him and pulls him into her arms, hugging her to him. "I love you. SO much."

I squat down next to them and Holland throws her arms around my neck. "Yes, I will be your wife, Reed Davidson," she cries.

Taking the box from Evan, I remove the oval-shaped diamond and slide it on to her shaking ring finger. Then, I hold my fist out for Evan to bump.

"We did it, bud."

His little fist hits mine then he says, "Can I have ice cream now?"

Holland and I both laugh.

"Yes, bud, let's get some ice cream. Go tell Mr. Bert bye and I'll be waiting for you when you get back."

Evan nods and takes off toward the fence line.

Holland looks over at me, still holding her hand up to stare at the ring that Em helped me choose for her. "I can't believe I get to marry you."

"I can't wait. How's tomorrow sound?"

She throws her head back and laughs. "You never do anything slowly, do you?"

"Remember how we got here?"

"I wouldn't trade it for anything in the world."

While we're waiting for Evan to come back, my phone buzzes over and over in my pocket, and when I finally pull it out to check what's happening, there's a dozen texts with the last one from Briggs saying:

Briggs: @ the hospital, COME NOW EMERGENCY.

Holland reads it and her eyes widen. "Oh god, we need to go. What has he gotten himself into now?"

That, baby… is the million-dollar question.

What has Briggs Wilson done now?

Thank you for reading Reed & Holland's book! Next up for the delicious Puck Daddies of Chicago is… Briggs in *Sincerely, The Puck Bunny.*

Gossip girl…. Meets the NHL.

A secret baby, hockey romance you do **NOT** want to miss.

ALSO BY MAREN MOORE

Standalone:

The Enemy Trap

The Newspaper Nanny

Totally Pucked Series:

Change on the Fly

Sincerely, The Puck Bunny

The Scorecard

Playboy Playmaker

The Penalty Shot

TURN THE PAGE FOR A SNEAK PEEK INTO THE ENEMY TRAP, AVAILABLE NOW!

MAREN MOORE

CHAPTER ONE
SOPHIA

It seems fitting that I'm ringing in the dreaded big "three-oh" wine drunk on my couch in granny panties and a semi fashionable muumuu. Honestly, if that isn't a birds-eye view of my life, then I don't know what is.

I'm not just a little drunk—I'm a lotta drunk. Like, call your ex and cry on the phone, professing your love for him—even though he cheated on you with your cousin—kind of drunk. Trust me, I hope I forget it by the time morning rolls around.

Highly, highly unlikely.

"Soph, are you listening?" my best friend Holly asks. She's sitting on the arm of my hot pink loveseat, engrossed in the sub-par job she's doing of painting her toes candy apple red.

"Umm, no. Sorry, I was reliving the word vomit that just spewed from my mouth," I groan, dropping my head into my hands. This is not how I envisioned the whole "death to my twenties" party. But that's what happens when you're the last of your single friends. Everyone's married and has kids, and I'll forever be stuck being the cool aunt.

"Tell me again why I thought it would be a good idea to call him? This is going to suck a lot more when I'm hungover and semi clear-headed."

Holly shrugs. "I have no clue why you do half the shit you do, Soph. But...I said, Scott and I made a sex schedule. You know, with Brady teething and Gracie in dance, we really wanted to nail down a time." She grins, "Get it, nail? No, but seriously, how boring and predictable is my life that we have to schedule sex. I've officially reached my peak. It's only downhill from here."

"At least you have someone to have sex with and who wants to have sex with you."

She finally looks up from her toes and rolls her eyes, "Yes, sixty seconds of missionary and a faked orgasm is honestly something to look forward to."

Okay, she had a point. Still, I'd take a fake orgasm over none at all.

"Ugh, if you'd stop dating guys like Horndog Harry, this wouldn't be a problem." Her tone softens when she sees my expression, a mixture of hurt and regret, "I just hate to see you get hurt over and over by the same types of guys—scared of commitment and couldn't keep his dick in his pants if his life depended on it. Honestly, I don't know what the appeal is with him. You are definitely a ten, and he's like...a three, at best."

"It's not like I purposefully attract assholes, Hol! Apparently, I have a sign on my forehead that says "Please fuck me up." And I'm a solid seven, not a ten."

She rolls her eyes and stands abruptly, setting down the nail polish on my second-hand coffee table and stomping over to where I sit dejectedly on the arm of the couch. At five-eight, she towers over me. Her dark hair is always ten kinds of hot mess, but she pulls it off flawlessly. Holly is the only person I know who could have six days of unwashed hair, dark bags under her eyes, be wearing the same shirt as yesterday, and still look like a supermodel straight off the cover of Vogue. It's ridiculously unfair.

"Listen, enough of this sad bullshit. It's your birthday—we're celebrating, not crying into our beers."

"We're drinking wine..." I squint at her, trying to figure out where she's going with this.

"Whatever. You get it. Oh! Wait," she snaps her fingers, "I've got an idea. I know exactly what you need to cheer you up, and it'll be a stepping stone in the path of getting over HH and under someone else."

Here we go.

I drain my wine in one long gulp that seems to go on forever. My head spins as I swallow down the alcohol, but screw it, I'm in. In like Flynn...

She disappears into my room and comes back moments later holding the box of photos I have stashed under my bed that I wasn't even aware she knew about.

"You hussy, how did you even know about those?

Holly rolls her eyes, "Because you're a sentimental bitch. But, no longer! We're burning this shit, and you're going to enjoy every single second of it. Goodbye to the little dick, shitty cheater of a fiancé, and hello to a brand new Sophia St. James. You're hot, single, and a solid nine.

She smirks, holding out the box and shaking it back and forth with a shimmy, as if to entice me.

What could it hurt? Maybe it'll help me let go of some of the anger I've been holding in. Lord knows I'm drunk enough to forget it in the morning.

"Fine."

I take the box from her and remove the lid. Maybe she's right; maybe it is time to let go of the past and move forward. Harry doesn't deserve me, and he obviously deserves my slut/homewrecking whore of a cousin. Those two are a match made in heaven. If anything, my cousin did me a favor.

"I need something harder for this. Jose, my darling, come to me," I sing-song, dancing over to the fridge.

Don't judge me. I'm going to drown my sorrow in the only man who will never break my heart.

This conversation is making me think too much about my sad, boring life. I'm stuck in the same town I grew up in: same people, same faces, same places.

Broke. Thirty. And single... Probably forever.

I had every reason to cry into my beer. Wine. Bottle of tequila. Whatever.

"Alright, I've decided," I tell Holly as she's rifling through my junk drawer for a lighter. "One more night of feeling sorry for myself, and then I'm going to put my big girl panties on, go back to the foundation, ask for my job back, apologize for my momentary lapse in judgment, and grow up. I mean, I'm thirty, " I whisper, like it's a secret I want no one to hear.

You see, I might have fallen off the deep end a tiny, minuscule amount when I found out I was being cheated on—I quit my job and wallowed on the couch for two weeks straight until Holly came over, fumigated my apartment, and made me shower.

It's not that I hate my job per se, but I feel stuck. Like I'm never going to be anything more than I am right now.

The boring job, the cheating fiancé, the backstabbing friends. Turning thirty is really making me open my eyes and see the bigger picture.

Okay, so it's only been like three hours, but still. I'm a changed woman.

"Got it! Let's go." She thrusts the lighter at me and grabs my hand, pulling me out the backdoor, even though I'm in a muumuu that barely covers my ass, "Wait, I want pictures of this as you literally send the old you up in flames. Like a phoenix rising from the fucking ashes, Soph."

Jesus, why did I agree to this? She is entirely too excited to light shit on fire.

Together, we light the photos and watch the memories blaze. The fire crackles and pops as it destroys a part of my life I'm not all that sorry to see go. Holly's right...I do feel lighter. Maybe it's the fact that I know this box is no longer going to be stuffed under my bed, waiting for me to pull the photos out and relive the memories over and over again. Or, maybe it's the fact that HH is a douchebag, and deep down I've always known it—I just never wanted to admit it. Catching him with Emily wasn't surprising, at least not now, after the fact. I should've seen the signs.

I should've realized that I was a ten and he was a six, at best.

And that's not just my man Jose talking.

"To stupid assholes who cheat and break our hearts, only to make us stronger." Holly raises the bottle of tequila and takes a sip, her face scrunching in distaste as it burns going down.

"You're married Hol. Happily, remember?" I laugh, snatching the bottle from her.

"This is about you, not me." Linking her arm in mine, she drags me back towards the house. "Now that you've let go of the past, it's time to move forward. We're setting you up with a dating profile and finding you Mr. Right. We'll think of a good bio that screams, "Crazy, but not crazy enough to slash your tires." Guys love crazy bitches. Trust me."

"Uh, no. Absolutely not."

"Really? What happened to the brave, bad ass, solid ten Sophia that just burned every memory of her piece of shit ex? Go take a shower; you've got ashes in your hair. Symbolic, I'm telling ya."

Half a bottle of tequila and a lot of tears later, my still delicate, broken heart lay in tatters on the floor. Add in a shower, more tears, and another signature muumuu, snuggled on the couch with my best friend, and it's a birthday I'll never forget.

The beginning of a new chapter in the messy book of my life.

"Oh, hell," Holly breathes, looking at her phone like it's grown two heads.

"What?"

She flips the phone around, showing me the screen.

I groan.

On the screen is the very person I despise more than HH, and that's saying a lot. Hayes Davis.

Of course, it's another gossip magazine and another scandal. The guy got himself in more shit than a Kardashian.

"You have got to be kidding me. Does he want to destroy his career? Is being a rich professional hockey player not enough for him? Gross. I mean, not that I keep up with him or anything, but he's on the cover of a different magazine every week with a new scandal in hand."

Holly gives me a knowing smile. "You know, he was voted Hollywood's Most Eligible Bachelor this year."

"Gross. Hope they had a spot for his enormous ego too."

"Yep. He called Scott last week to talk to him about it. Those two gossip on the phone more than we do."

I gag, sticking my finger down my throat for dramatic effect.

"Out of every guy in the world, they chose him. Didn't their mamas teach them that looks are deceiving?"

She rolls her eyes, "You two are ridiculous. Neither of you have moved on since high school."

"Well, that's because...because he's...Hayes Davis! Arrogant. Egotistical. Vain as they come. Ringing a bell? He is Scott's best friend, and for whatever reason, your kids' godfather. You should be well aware of how vile he is."

"Well, unfortunately, the world seems to disagree. Introducing Mr. Hollywood's Most Eligible Bachelor." She grins.

Hayes Davis. America's sweetheart, and my number one enemy. Yep, even over HH and his cheating pencil dick.

I'd rather use cardboard tampons than spend another second of my time talking about him.

"No, but really, you guys would be so cute together, Soph. Maybe it's time you stop fake hating him and let Scott and I hook you up. He's hot—you can't deny it. Remember, we're leaving the past in the past?"

"Hol! He's your husband's best friend." I cry, my eyes wide.

Shrugging, she looks back at her computer, "So? He is on People's Sexiest Men Alive list, so it's merely an observation of fact."

"Too bad they don't account for how big egos are when they choose them, or Hayes would be screwed. I think he's making up for what he lacks in dick size."

"Sophia St. James, you are so hot for him. Stop lying."

Another gag, and I'm five seconds from puking on my Goodwill couch. Hot pink velvet and puke do not mix. I can think of at least ten torture activities I'd prefer over being in the same room with Hayes. Thankfully, even though he's Scott's best friend, he's busy warming every puck bunny's bed from here to Seattle, so I rarely have to be subjected to seeing him.

Only for the kids' birthdays and the occasional holiday, which is more than enough for me. The less the better.

I didn't like to give Scott shit about it since we were all adults, and I really should be over the whole number one enemy from childhood thing, but...I'm a huge grudge holder, so I'm not getting over this anytime soon.

It doesn't help that the few times Hayes does come home, he flaunts his money and a new bimbo on his arm. Not that I would ever—and I mean ever—admit it out loud, but he was ridiculously attractive, to the point that I wanted to punch him in the balls just for being so insanely handsome.

No one should be that perfect on the outside and so ugly on the inside. Life can be so unfair sometimes.

"I'd rather you run me over with your car than touch Hayes."

"Dramatic. Whatever. It was just an idea. It's time to put yourself back out there, Soph. It's been over six months since HH. Can we please put you on the dating site? Just give it a shot. If it sucks, you can delete your profile."

"Dating sites are gross. A giant waste of time. I already tried it, and it was a shitshow. Everyone pretends to be someone they aren't just to match with someone. Remember that time I met the guy who brought his mother? He paid more attention to her than me."

She squints her nose when she remembers that date. "Okay,

true. But that was just one. You can't let one ruin it for them all."

"Okay…What about the guy who sucked his thumb…at thirty? Oh, or what about the one who recorded all our conversations so he could replay them later?"

"Alright. Fine. No dating sites. But, at least give your number to that guy from yoga. He was super hot."

I shake my head. "And he also likes the same guys that I do, Hol. Stop playing matchmaker. I'm fine being alone. Actually, I'm thriving being single, free, and happy with myself. Really."

"Whatever you say, Soph."

Okay, I was lying. We both knew it. I hated being alone. I preferred to be in a relationship, however comfortable it was, even if sex was scheduled. I'd choose that over waking up each morning alone.

"Fine. I was lying."

"I know."

"One dating site. One. And not the Singles in Seattle one. That one was full of weirdos. Oh, what about this one?" I point to Tinder.

"Yes!" She squeals, clicking on the signup button. "You're going to meet the man of your dreams, just watch. When you least expect it, Mr. Perfect is going to sweep in and sweep you off your feet."

Famous last words, if there ever were any.

ACKNOWLEDGEMENTS

Everyone always asks me what is my favorite part about writing a book, and while there are so many things that I love about publishing, this part is my favorite.

Giving the credit where it's really due. Because without these people, I wouldn't be who I am. I wouldn't be able to publish or write, and I can never thank them enough for the sacrifices they've made.

To my best friend in the world, Holly Renee. I love you. Words are useless when it comes to how I feel. Soul sisters for life.

To Jac, I could write an entire book about how much you mean to me, but I just hope you know that I love you unconditionally and I cherish you.

Katie, this book would not exist without you. Period. That is a fact. You held my hand, and pushed me when I thought I couldn't finish. I owe everything to you. I love you.

To my author friends who continually support, encourage, and offer guidance…. I treasure each and every one of you. You are a light in my life. All of the Savage Queens (literally all of you lol!) Trilina Pucci, Meagan Brandy, Giana Darling, CoraLee June, Alley Ciz, SJ Sylvis, Julia Wolf, Shantel Tessier, Samantha Lind, Eliah Greenwood, Amanda Richardson and so many more. Love you girls.

To Alex, Haley and Jan for being my alphas and betas. Your advice is so critical to my writing. I couldn't do it without you. I love you each SO much.

To my amazing publicist Amanda who I really don't deserve. Thank you for all of your hard work and your friendship. I CANNOT LIVE WITHOUT YOU AMANDA. Okay? Love you.

To my street team, and to my Facebook group Give Me Moore. Thank you for all of the hard work that you do. You share, repost, comment and hype my books and it is so very much appreciated.

And as always, thank you to the readers and bloggers who pick this up and take a chance on me. Whether you loved or hated it, the fact that you took the chance means everything. Without you, our world wouldn't turn.

CHANGE ON THE FLY

CHANGE ON THE FLY